Joel Parker

The Domestic and Foreign Relations of the United States

Joel Parker

The Domestic and Foreign Relations of the United States

ISBN/EAN: 9783337723101

Printed in Europe, USA, Canada, Australia, Japan

Cover: Foto ©Andreas Hilbeck / pixelio.de

More available books at **www.hansebooks.com**

THE

DOMESTIC AND FOREIGN RELATIONS

OF THE

UNITED STATES.

By JOEL PARKER.

———————

CAMBRIDGE:
WELCH, BIGELOW, AND COMPANY,
PRINTERS TO THE UNIVERSITY.
1862.

MEMORANDUM. — The substance of the first part of the following Tract was
contained in a Lecture delivered to the students in the Law School of Harvard
College, by the author, as Royall Professor of Law in that Institution, on the 25th
of June, 1861. Subsequent events have led to an enlargement of it, and to its
publication in the January number of the North American Review. It is now
issued as a separate Article, a single paragraph being omitted because it was little
more than a repetition of what was expressed elsewhere, and some Notes being
added in an Appendix.

CAMBRIDGE, *January* 1, 1862.

THE DOMESTIC AND FOREIGN RELATIONS

OF THE

UNITED STATES.

It may be stated as a result of our examination of the alleged Right of Secession, that the people of the several States composing the United States, under the Constitution, — whether that instrument be regarded as an organic law, or as a compact, — form an entire Nation, for the purposes for which they are thus united; while under their State organizations they exercise many powers of sovereignty, of a political and municipal character, some of which are subordinate to the powers of the General government, and others independent of that government because they do not fall within the scope of the purposes for which it was organized, and all "powers not delegated to the United States by the Constitution, nor prohibited by it to the States, are reserved to the States respectively, or to the people."

This nation has, for the accomplishment of the objects of its existence, all the attributes of sovereignty. The Constitution — providing that itself shall be the supreme law of the land, and binding upon all the judges of the several States, anything in the constitution or laws of any State to the contrary notwithstanding; requiring all the legislators, and executive and judicial officers of the United States, and of the several States, to take an oath or affirmation to support it; and defining what shall constitute treason against the United States—shows that, so far as the objects and purposes of the national government extend, an allegiance is due to that government from all the citizens within its limits, paramount to and exclusive of any allegiance due to the several States ; because the allegiance to the State arises under the State organization and constitution, which, to the extent covered by the Constitution of the United States, are subordinate to the authority of the United States, under that Constitution. There can be, therefore, no right on the part of any State, or of the people of any State, through or by any State authority or action, or by any popular vote, to terminate this allegiance to the United States.

The Union under the Constitution being perpetual and indissoluble, it is to be subverted only by the exercise of the right of revolution, for sufficient cause. And this right of revolution is a personal, and not a State right, and of an imperfect character; for an attempt at revolution is legally, in its inception, and until it is attended with success, neither more nor less than rebellion against the existing government, which of course has at least an equal right to resist the attempt by all the forces at its command. It follows, therefore, that those persons who have been active in the attempted secession of the several States have, as respects the United States, no authority derived from any State organization ; nor any exemption, through the color of any exercise of State authority, from the ordinary consequences which attach to an insurrection or rebellion. No convention of the people of a State could confer any authority to resist the government of the United States, in the full exercise of its functions, in all of its departments, legislative, executive, and judicial ; and still less could any act of a State legislature give any color of legal authority for such resistance, whether such legislature assumed to act under the State constitution as it existed before the attempted secession, or under the authority of a convention which, having declared the secession, assumed to confer new legislative powers, or to adopt a new constitution. All persons who have placed themselves in hostility to the United States by acts of war, are of course responsible personally for those acts, as rebels and traitors. The State which they assume to represent is not responsible, because the State, as a State, did not, and could not, in any mode, give authority to commit acts of rebellion and treason. There is no war between any State, admitted into the Union, and the United States; because the State itself — the legal, constitutionally organized State — is not in rebellion; and there is therefore no authority to confiscate the property of any State, as State property, for any such State offence. The persons who have seized upon the State organization for the purposes of rebellion, and who wield an apparent State authority for such purposes, — who have, moreover, created a confederation under this usurpation, and style themselves governors and senators, generals and captains, president and secretaries, — are in no manner shielded by their titles or offices from the punishment due to their acts of treason, which are, in fact, in more senses than one, committed on private account.

This serves to show that the proclamation of President Lincoln, treating the seizure of forts, arsenals, and dock-yards, and the bombardment of Fort Sumter, as acts of insurrection, and requiring those concerned in them to retire peaceably to their respective abodes, was not only in precise accordance with the requisition of the statute of 1795, but was founded upon the only correct legal view of the existing state of things which called it forth. The acts of hostility against the government had, perhaps, assumed such formidable proportions as to be appropriately designated as war; but it was a war of persons owing allegiance to the general or national government, and not a war of governments. Those acts were not more than acts of treason because millions were engaged in them, and they were not less than acts of treason because of the assumed titles, military and civil, or of the assumption of

State or Confederate authority, under color of which they were committed. There were millions of people in India engaged in a war against the government of Great Britain, within a short period; and most of them acted under the orders of persons who stood to them in the relation of kings and princes, for certain purposes, having recognized authority for such purposes, but who had no authority for the objects and purposes of such a war; and they were all, kings, princes, and sepoys, held alike as rebels against the paramount government, — their guilt differing only in degree, according to the circumstances of enormity attending it. We do not inquire into the causes of that revolt, when we consider the case in its political and legal aspects in regard to the United States. That is a matter between the persons engaged in it and Great Britain. The government of the United States has nothing to dread from such an inquiry, in the present instance; but other nations will not enter into that inquiry, and it is foreign to our immediate purpose.

We perceive, therefore, that the criticism upon the proclamation of the President requiring the rebels to disperse, that it addressed its command in fact to millions, and that it was preposterous to require such large numbers, like an ordinary mob, to retire to their places of abode; and that other criticism which assumed that the States were the actors in the warfare which was waged, and that the statute and the proclamation could not apply, because the States had no abodes to retire to, — fail entirely of their intended force. Rebels may form political associations for themselves, and may assume to have a government for which they ask and claim recognition. They may, as between themselves, wield the powers of a State government, if they can usurp the State authority, and use it as if they were the rightful possessors of it. They may thus have a government *de facto*, and it may be, as among themselves, *de jure* also. But all this does not change their legal relations to the government against which they are in arms, until they have by their power accomplished the purpose of the insurrection, by a practical maintenance of their assumed independence.

We deduce from these premises the conclusion, that, as regards the United States, there is no right in any organization which these rebels and traitors have constituted — whether designated as State or Confederation — to enact a law, or to adopt an ordinance, which shall be recognized by the United States as having force or effect as a legal enactment, or as conferring upon any person power to be used in hostility to the existing government. There can be no lawful confederation of the States involved in the attempted secession, because there has been no secession of those States which is recognized as having any validity. They still remain as component parts of the United States, having doubtless a large loyal population, although the violence of the insurgents has for a time suspended the due exercise of the authority of the United States, and that of the State also, by a usurpation of the powers of the latter, and an exercise of the semblance of authority under the State organization. As States in the Union, the Constitution expressly forbids any confederation among them ; and for that reason also, if there had been no insurrection, and no attempt to array State authority against the national government, the confederation of the States would be unconstitutional ; the self-styled Congress of the Confederate States an unauthorized body ; and the so-called President of that confederation, and his cabinet councillors, suitable subjects for the criminal jurisprudence of the United States, on an indictment for a conspiracy, — if their acts of war had not made them liable to the graver penalty attached to treason.

As a necessary consequence of all this, the proclamation of Mr. Jefferson Davis, calling himself President of the Confederate States, in which he invited applications for letters of marque and reprisal against the United States, — or, in other words, in a legal view, Mr. Davis's advertisement for proposals to rob, under his sanction, such citizens of the United States as might have property afloat, — was no better than the advertisement of any other private person; and the letters of marque and reprisal issued by him as President, and countersigned by R. Toombs as if he were a Secretary of State, are, as respects the United States, no better than so much waste paper, for the justification and protection of those who capture property under them. Such persons are amenable to the laws of the United States as pirates, under the act of Congress of 1790, Chapter 9.

The eighth section of that statute provides that, " if any person or persons shall commit upon the high seas, or in any river, haven, basin, or bay out of the jurisdiction of any particular State, murder or robbery, or any other offence which, if committed within the body of a county, would by the laws of the United States be punishable with death ; . . . . . every such offender shall be deemed, taken, and adjudged to be a pirate and felon, and, being thereof convicted, shall suffer death." The ninth section enacts that, " if any citizen shall commit any piracy or robbery aforesaid, or any act of hostility against the United States, or any citizen thereof, upon the high sea, under color of any commission from any foreign prince or state, or on pretence of authority from any person, such offender shall, notwithstanding the pretence of any such authority, be deemed, adjudged, and taken to be a pirate, felon, and robber, and on being thereof convicted shall suffer death."

The insurgents are not absolved from responsibility under this statute by the fact that their offences were committed in the course of what in other aspects may have the character of war, nor by the fact that they have been taken prisoners in that war.

Martens admits the right of the conqueror to take the lives of prisoners in three cases: —

" 1. When sparing their lives is inconsistent with his own safety;

2. in cases where he has the right to exercise the *talio* or to make reprisals; 3. when the crime committed by those who fall into his hands justifies the taking of their lives." — *Summary of the Law of Nations,* Chap. 3, Sect. 4.

Vattel concedes a right to punish prisoners who have been personally guilty of some crime against the captor.

" Prisoners may be secured, and, for this purpose, they may be put into confinement, and even fettered if there be reason to apprehend that they will rise upon their captors or make their escape. But they are not to be treated harshly, unless personally guilty of some crime against him who has them in his power. In this case he is at liberty to punish them; otherwise he should remember that they are men, and unfortunate." — Book III. Chap. 8, Sect. 150.

It is by no means clear that those who come under the condemnation of this statute of 1790 by acts of force and plunder on board the Confederate privateers, would not be liable to the same condemnation under the rules of public law; for although a pirate is generally described as *hostis humani generis*, because the buccaneer ordinarily makes war indiscriminately upon the vessels of all nations, yet if a band of sea-robbers should confine their depredations to the commerce of a single nation, it would seem that, as to that nation, their crime might well be regarded as piracy, even if other nations whose commerce was not assailed did not so regard it.

It may be asked wherein consists the material difference between persons who act under a privateer's commission, and capture property on the high seas, and those who wage war upon the land, and commit homicide, and burn, destroy, or capture property there. Why should the former when taken be held and treated as pirates, and the others when captured held and exchanged as prisoners of war? It is a sufficient answer to this to say, that the war of the privateer is mainly upon the property of private persons, by private parties, for their private emolument. If the privateer attack a public vessel, it is the exception, and not the rule ; she is not commissioned with that view. On the other hand, the war of the land forces is of a more public character, such as fighting battles offensive or defensive, assaults upon forts and batteries, and the like, and their interference with private property is usually incidental to those more direct and public operations. The object of the hostilities waged by privateers is mainly gain, by the plunder of commercial vessels ; the injury done to the enemy being only incidental to that object. The object of the military operations upon land is ordinarily the public object of the war, whatever that may be, the injury done to private property being incidental to the measures taken for that purpose. If, then, the hostilities of the privateer are not regarded as war under lawful authority, they have the character of private acts, to wit, murder and robbery.

Letters of marque and reprisal were originally granted to merchants who had lost goods by capture, in order that they might indemnify themselves by capture of the property of subjects of the offending nation. They were, and may still be, used before a war, as a means of procuring justice for a wrong or injury sustained by a nation, its citizens or subjects ; but a resort to this measure presupposes the existence of such wrong or injury.

" When a nation cannot obtain justice, whether for a wrong or an injury, she has a right to do herself justice. But before she declare war (of which we shall treat in the following Book), there are various methods practised among nations, which remain to be treated of here. Among those methods of obtaining satisfaction has been reckoned what is called the law of retaliation, according to which we make another suffer precisely as much evil as he has done. . . . . .

" Let us say, then, that a nation may punish another which has done her an injury, as we have shown above (see Chap. IV. and VI. of this Book), if the latter refuses to give a just satisfaction ; but she has not a right to extend the penalty beyond what her own safety requires. Retaliation, which is unjust between private persons, would be much more so between nations, because it would, in the latter case, be difficult to make the punishment fall on those who had done the injury. What right have you to cut off the nose and ears of the ambassador of a barbarian who had treated your ambassador in that manner? As to those reprisals in time of war which partake of the nature of retaliation, they are justified on other principles; and we shall speak of them in their proper place." — *Vattel,* Book II. Chap. XVIII. Sect. 339.

" Reprisals are used between nation and nation, in order to do themselves justice when they cannot otherwise obtain it. If a nation has taken possession of what belongs to another, — if she refuses to pay a debt, to repair an injury, or to give adequate satisfaction for it, — the latter may seize something belonging to the former, and apply it to her own advantage till she obtains payment of what is due to her, together with interest and damages, — or keep it as a pledge till she has received ample satisfaction." — *Ibid.,* Sect. 342.

" There are cases, however, in which reprisals would be justly condemnable, even when a declaration of war would not be so ; and these are precisely those cases in which nations may with justice take up arms. When the question which constitutes the ground of a dispute relates, not to an·act of violence, or an injury received, but to a contested right, — after an ineffectual endeavor to obtain justice by conciliatory and pacific measures, it is a declaration of war that ought to follow, and not pretended reprisals, which, in such a case, would only be real acts of hostility, without a declaration of war, and would be contrary to public faith, as well as to the mutual duties of nations." — *Ibid.,* Sect. 354.

" Reprisals by commission, or letters of marque and reprisal, granted to one or more injured subjects, in the name and by the authority of a sovereign, is another mode of redress for some specific injury, which is considered to be compatible with a state of peace, and permitted by the law of nations. The case arises when one nation has committed some direct and palpable injury to another, as by withholding a just debt, or by violence to person or property, and has refused to give any satisfaction." — 1 *Kent's Comm.* 61.

The principle stated in these authorities relates to reprisals as a measure of redress before the existence of a war. But when reprisals are resorted to in time of war, for the purpose of weakening the enemy by depriving his subjects or citizens of their property, the principle that there can be no lawful reprisals until an injury is sustained is equally applicable.

Wheaton enumerates, "among the various modes of terminating the differences between nations by forcible means short of actual war," —

4. "By making reprisals upon the persons and things belonging to the offending nation, until a satisfactory reparation is made for the alleged injury."

He says : —

" Reprisals are also *general* or *special*. They are *general* when a state which has received, or supposes it has received, an injury from another nation, delivers commissions to its officers and subjects to take the persons and property belonging to the other nation, wherever the same may be found. It is, according to present usage, the first step which is usually taken at the commencement of a public war, and may be considered as amounting to a declaration of hostilities, unless satisfaction is made by the offending state. *Special* reprisals are where letters of marque are granted, in time of peace, to particular individuals who have suffered an injury from the government or subjects of another nation."

" Reprisals are to be granted only in case of a clear and open denial of justice." — *Elements of Int. Law*, Part IV. Chap. I. Sect. 1, 2.

It is one of the singular features, however, of this controversy and warfare, and one of the strange perversions of all ordinary action, that the proposals by Mr. Jefferson Davis to issue " letters of marque and *reprisal* " were made before any article of property belonging to the Confederate States, or any one of them, or to any person claiming to be a citizen of any one of those States, had been interfered with ; or any person belonging to the Confederate States had been molested by the government of the United States, except in self-defence.* It is true that the United States in the war of 1812, by the same

---

act in which they declared the existence of the war, authorized the President to issue letters of marque and reprisal ; but
it must be recollected that they complained of long-continued
grievances by reason of the seizure of men and property, the
confiscation of property, and the denial of reparation. The
cases are not only unlike ; they are entirely dissimilar. The
Confederate States can hardly claim to make reprisals because
of the passage of a tariff long since repealed, even supposing
it to have been onerous ; or the passage of personal-liberty
laws by some of the States ; or the refusal of Congress to as-
sent that slavery should be admitted into the Territories ; or
the election of Mr. Lincoln. None of these things were done
to, or suffered by, the Confederate States, which were not then
in existence as a belligerent power, or in separation from the
United States. In the war of the Revolution, the United Colonies did not attempt to authorize the capture of private property until nearly a year after the commencement of hostilities.
Not so the Secessionists. There is no doubt that, from the
first, even before any vote of secession, this warfare upon private property was relied upon as one of the means of insuring
the success of the insurrection. " If you do not let us secede
without any attempt at coercion, we will refuse to pay our
debts, and, by means of privateers, ruin your commerce."

From what has been thus stated, we draw a further conclusion that the recent order of Mr. Judah P. Benjamin, acting
Secretary of War for the Confederate States, subjecting Colonels
Corcoran, Wood, and Lee, Major Revere, and others, who were
taken prisoners by the Confederate forces at the battle of Ball's
Bluff, to imprisonment in the dungeons of felons, in retaliation or reprisal for the imprisonment of persons taken prisoners on board of the Confederate privateers, some of whom have
been tried for piracy under the statute of the United States
before cited, is a gross violation of the rules of honorable warfare. The Confederates attempt to escape from the odium of
treason by alleging the existence of war. They are bound,

then, to conduct the warfare on their part according to the usages of civilized nations. But there is no usage of nations by which one belligerent, having prisoners who have never been amenable to its laws, and have committed no crime against them, but who have been taken in battle fighting under their own banners, can immure those persons in damp dungeons, and subject them to the treatment of convicts, merely because its belligerent adversary, finding among his prisoners those who according to his laws owe allegiance, and have committed treason, or who in violation of long-existing statutes have incurred the guilt of piracy, proceeds with such persons in the ordinary course of justice according to those laws. If one belligerent merely proceeds according to law, that furnishes no reason why the other should resort to measures sanctioned by no law. The law of reprisals, as it affects persons, — usually termed retaliation, or *lex talionis*, — may rightfully be resorted to in time of war by one nation, when a gross outrage in violation of the laws of war has been committed upon its citizens or subjects by the other, in order to restrain and prevent further outrage. Some of the accredited writers upon public and natural law will, however, hardly sustain even this proposition.

Rutherforth expressly denies the right of retaliation by killing prisoners, when the enemy has done the same thing : —

" The exceptions to this rule of not killing these persons, who never were in arms at all, or who, though they have been in arms, have surrendered themselves, are very few. If they are considered as members of the nation with which we are at war, nothing more is necessary, in the first instance, than to get them into our power. The law of nature, therefore, will not allow us to go further. But if they whom we thus get into our power have been guilty of any previous crime for which they deserve death, this law does not forbid us to inflict this punishment, any more than if they and we were members of no society at all, but were still in the original state of nature.

" The obstinacy of holding out long in a siege, is not one of these crimes; for a discharge of their duty towards their own nation is not in its own nature a crime against the other. There might, perhaps, be some advantage in putting a garrison to the sword for holding out long, as such an example might be a means to deter others from giving the besiegers the same trouble; but neither this nor any other motive of mere utility will render it just to take away the lives of those who are in our power, and have not deserved to lose them. Neither is retaliation a justifiable cause for killing prisoners of war. Though our adversaries should have killed the prisoners whom they have taken from us, this will not justify us in killing the prisoners whom we have taken from them. The law of nature allows of retaliation only where they who have done harm are made to suffer as much harm as they have done. But to kill such prisoners of war as are in our power, because the nation to which they belong has treated our countrymen in this manner, would be to do harm to one person because harm had been done by another. An injury which is done by a nation does, indeed, communicate itself to all the members of that nation; and such a communication of guilt is all that can be pleaded for the retaliation of which we have been speaking. But Grotius very truly replies here, that to punish captives or prisoners of war in this manner would be to punish them in what is their own as individuals, whereas the national guilt can only be communicated to them as they are members of the offending nation; and consequently the proper punishment of it should only be inflicted on them as they are members of the offending nation, and not as they are individuals." — *Institutes of Natural Law*, Book II. Chap. 9, Sect. 15.

"Prisoners of war are, indeed, sometimes killed; but this is no otherwise justifiable than as it is made necessary, either by themselves, if they make use of force against those who have taken them, or by others, who make use of force in their behalf, and render it impossible to keep them. And as we may collect from the reason of the thing, so it likewise appears, from common opinion, that nothing but the strongest necessity will justify such an act; for the civilized and thinking part of mankind will hardly be persuaded not to condemn it till they see the absolute necessity of it." — *Ibid.*

Martens admits a more extended rule. Under the head of Reprisals, he says: —

" A sovereign violates his perfect obligations in violating the natural or perfect rights of another. It matters not whether these rights are innate, or whether they have been acquired by express or tacit covenant, or otherwise.

"In case of such violation, the injured sovereign may refuse to fulfil his perfect obligations towards the sovereign by whom he is injured, or towards the subjects of such sovereign. He may also have recourse to more violent means, till he has obliged the offending party to yield him satisfaction, or till he has taken such satisfaction himself, and guarded himself against the like injuries in future.

" There are many acts by which a sovereign refuses to do or to suffer what he is perfectly obliged to do or to suffer, or by which he does what he is ordinarily obliged to omit, in order to obtain satisfaction for a real injury sustained. All these acts are called reprisals. Consequently, reprisals are of many sorts. The *talio*, by which an injury received is returned by an injury exactly equal to it, is one sort of re-prisals ; but the use of it is not indiscriminately permitted on all occasions." — *Law of Nations*, Book VIII. Chap. 1, Sect. 3.

In a note he adds : —

" If the ambassador or messenger of a state has been put to death by another state, the former state could not, on that account, have a right to put the ambassador or messenger of the latter to death ; but in time of war, a prisoner of war may sometimes be put to death in order to punish a nation that has violated the laws of war. In the first case, the injured nation has other means of obtaining satisfaction, and of guarding against such violations for the future ; but war being of itself the last state of violence, there often remains no other means of guarding against future violations on the part of the enemy."

So Vattel admits the right to execute prisoners in retaliation for an execution by the hostile general without any just reason, and against an inhuman enemy who frequently commits enormities.

" This leads us to speak of a kind of retaliation sometimes practised in war, under the name of reprisals. If the hostile general has, without any just reason, caused some prisoners to be hanged, we hang an equal number of his people, and of the same rank, — notifying to him that we will continue thus to retaliate, for the purpose of obliging him to observe the laws of war. It is a dreadful extremity thus to condemn a prisoner to atone, by a miserable death, for his general's crime; and if we had previously promised to spare the life of that prisoner, we cannot, without injustice, make him the subject of our reprisals. Nevertheless, as a prince or his general has a right to sacrifice his enemies' lives to his own safety and that of his men, it appears, that, if he has to do with an inhuman enemy, who frequently commits such enormities, he is authorized to refuse quarter to some of the prisoners he takes, and to treat them as his people have been treated." — Book III. Chap. 8, Sect. 142.

Chancellor Kent sums up the authorities in these words : —

" Cruelty to prisoners, and barbarous destruction of private property, will provoke the enemy to severe retaliation upon the innocent. Retaliation is said by Rutherforth not to be a justifiable cause for putting innocent prisoners or hostages to death; for no individual is chargeable, by the laws of nations, with the guilt of a personal crime, merely because the community of which he is a member is guilty. He is only responsible as a member of the state, in his property, for reparation in damages for the acts of others; and it is on this principle that, by the law of nations, private property may be taken and appropriated in war. Retaliation, to be just, ought to be confined to the guilty individuals, who may have committed some enormous violation of public law. On this subject of retaliation, Professor Martens is not so strict. While he admits that the life of an innocent man cannot be taken, unless in extraordinary cases, he declares that cases will sometimes occur, when the established usages of war are violated, and there are no other means, except the influence of retaliation, of restraining the enemy from further excesses. Vattel speaks of retaliation as a sad extremity, and it is frequently threatened without being put in execution, and probably without the intention to do it, and in hopes that fear will operate to restrain the enemy. Instances of resolutions to retaliate on innocent prisoners of war occurred in this country during the Revolutionary war, as well as during the war of 1812; but there was no instance in which retaliation beyond the measure of severe confinement took place in respect to prisoners of war." — *Commentaries*, I. 93, 94.

From the more recent work of Wheaton, we quote to the same effect.

" A belligerent has, therefore, no right to take away the lives of those subjects of the enemy whom he can subdue by any other means. Those who are actually in arms, and continue to resist, may be lawfully killed; but the inhabitants of the enemy's country, who are not in arms, or who, being in arms, submit and surrender themselves, may not be slain, because their destruction is not necessary for obtaining the just ends of war. Those ends may be accomplished by making prisoners of those who are taken in arms, or compelling them to give security that they will not bear arms against the victor for a limited period, or during the continuance of the war. The killing of prisoners can only be justifiable in those extreme cases where resistance on their part, or on the part of others who come to their rescue, renders it impossible to keep them. Both reason and general opinion concur in showing, that nothing but the strongest necessity will justify such an act." — *International Law*, Part IV. Chap. 2, Sect. 2.

" The exceptions to these general mitigations of the extreme rights of war, considered as a contest of force, all grow out of the same original principle of natural law, which authorizes us to use against an enemy such a degree of violence, and such only, as may be necessary to secure the objects of hostilities. The same general rule, which determines how far it is lawful to destroy the persons of enemies, will serve as a guide in judging how far it is lawful to ravage or lay waste their country. If this be necessary, in order to accomplish the just ends of war, it may be lawfully done, but not otherwise. Thus, if the progress of an enemy cannot be stopped, nor our own frontier secured, or if the approaches to a town, intended to be attacked, cannot be made without laying waste the intermediate territory, the extreme case may justify a resort to measures not warranted by the ordinary purposes of war. If modern usage has sanctioned any other exceptions, they will be found in the right of reprisals or vindictive retaliation. The whole international code is founded upon reciprocity. The rules it prescribes are observed by one nation, in confidence that they will be so by others. Where, then, the established usages of war are violated by an enemy, and there are no other means of restraining his excesses, retaliation may justly be resorted to by the suffering nation, in order to compel the

enemy to return to the observance of the law which he has violated."
— *Ibid.*, Sect. 6.

It is not astonishing, however, that those who violate all principle by the issue of letters of marque and reprisal when no injury has been done to them, and offer a premium of twenty dollars each for the destruction of persons on board any armed vessel of the United States sunk, burnt, or destroyed by a privateer of equal or inferior force, should imprison and threaten to hang other innocent persons, without any trial, merely because their adversary subjects those who accept and act under such commissions to plunder private property, and kill persons on the high seas, to an ordinary trial by jury for alleged offences committed against the laws of the government whose citizens are thus assailed.

But although the insurgents stand legally, as to the United States, in the position of rebels and traitors, and their privateersmen as pirates, and may be so held and treated, it is not a necessary result that the penalty should be exacted, nor that the warfare which exists should be carried on, in all respects, upon the assumption that the only *status* which can be assigned to them is that of rebels. An insurrection may, as we have seen, result in what is properly denominated a war, without losing its character as an insurrection, and without any exemption of those who participate in it from the penalties legally attached to rebellion. Such is the case with all civil wars which originate in an attempt to overthrow the existing government, or seek a separation from it. But in proportion to the magnitude and gravity of the warfare, it gradually loses, in the public mind, its distinctive character as an insurrection, being known as a civil war; and then it is hardly expedient to insist upon the enforcement of the extreme penalties of treason and piracy, against those who are merely subordinate and hireling agencies in wickedness. If such penalties are enforced at all, it should be against the active instigators of, and principals in, the rebellion; but these are the very offenders most likely to escape.

Great Britain, although she imprisoned several of the Colonists in the course of the war for Independence, and treated them thus far as rebels, did not in any case proceed to the extreme measure of execution.

When a rebellion is not immediately suppressed, but assumes the proportions and character of a war on the side of the insurgents, the parties to that war have necessarily, to a certain extent, the political character of belligerents. The government assailed must employ military forces, and place them in conflict with the military force arrayed against it; and the ordinary result of such conflict is the capture of prisoners on both sides. In the first stage of such a conflict, it may be just that the government assailed should treat its prisoners according to their legal *status* as traitors, or pirates, as one of the means of suppressing the insurrection. But when it is apparent that this means fails of its purpose, and becomes an unnecessary severity, the question immediately arises whether the government is not unjust to the persons whom it holds as captives, and who were mere subordinates in the hostilities which have been waged, if it refuse to extend to them the usual treatment of prisoners of war. And the more significant question follows, to wit, whether it is not guilty of still more gross injustice if it leave its own soldiers, who by misfortune have fallen into the hands of the other party, to the hardships of a captivity which it could terminate at any time by an exchange. That government which sends its soldiers into the field with the understanding that, if taken prisoners, they will be left to their fate, without an attempt to redeem them from the hardships and sufferings incident to such captivity, except by the ultimate success of the war, may thereby give them an additional incentive to fight unto death in any hopeless encounter in which they shall happen to be involved; but when it places itself on such a platform, it shows that it has little care for the comfort or safety of those who fight its battles. Certainly, an administration which should long conduct a war on that principle would not deserve to have battles fought for it.

An exchange of prisoners, while it is thus far a recognition, by implication, of a political *status* of the insurgents as an organized force, implies nothing respecting the legal character of that force. An exchange of prisoners may be made with an independent belligerent nation long established ; it may be made with a belligerent barbarian ; and so it may be made with insurgents, or even with those who are strictly pirates.

It seems clear that, while, on the one hand, the insurgents, by any amount of force which they can muster in the field, in giving to the contest the character of a war, cannot deprive the government assailed of the right to treat them as traitors ; so, on the other hand, government may voluntarily recognize the force arrayed against it as that of a belligerent party, against which it may adopt the modes of warfare usual among nations, as, for instance, a blockade, — or with which it may negotiate for the mitigation of the horrors and sufferings of the warfare, as by an exchange of prisoners, — without thereby depriving itself of the right still to hold the persons engaged in the insurrection as traitors or pirates, according to the nature and character of their hostile acts.

Regarding the Secessionists as mere insurgents and traitors, who by means of the insurrection have for the time subverted the legitimate authority of the United States, and deprived that government of the revenue from customs within the limits of the insurrection, — attempting at the same time to appropriate such revenue to their own use, — the government might, by a mere act or order, have closed the ports, as one of the means of suppressing the insurrection, instead of battering down the towns, which would, perhaps, be somewhat more effectual.. There seems to be no reasonable doubt that the President — who, under his power and duty to suppress the insurrection, might order the latter to be done, if in his judgment the exigency required it — might resort to the milder measure of interdicting all commerce there, when it became apparent that such commerce was not, and could not be, carried on with the United States, and, instead of being beneficial, was hostile to them. No blockading force is necessary to the validity of such an act or order. Each nation has a right, for its own reasons, to constitute and to abolish ports of entry; and one of the reasons for abolishing a port might be the existence of an insurrection there. And so long as other nations recognize the jurisdiction and authority of the government which abolishes, over the *locus in quo*, they must respect the act or order which denies entrance there, although it may be a mere paper regulation, without any military or naval force to support it. If, however, the abolishment of the port was in fact an act of hostility for the purpose of inflicting an injury upon another nation, instead of being designed as a municipal or domestic regulation, it might give just cause of offence.

But an act discontinuing a port of entry, or an order closing such a port and interdicting commerce there, is a very different matter from a blockade of the port. The term "blockade" has its appropriate signification. It means to block up, or shut up, — not to subvert or abolish; nor does it signify the closing of the port, except by the presence of a force for that purpose. A blockade, properly so called, while it may be used to suppress an insurrection, is not a mere measure for that purpose, without other incidents or consequences attached to it. A blockade proper imports the closing of the port of an enemy by a hostile power, thereby forbidding entrance and exit, under certain rules and limitations, and with certain exceptions; and it implies at the same time a right in other nations to enter and clear from the port, under the party in actual possession of it, if the blockade is not made effectual by a competent force. It is not the exercise of a mere municipal or domestic right, like that of closing a port by a repealing act, or an affirmative order for the purpose; but it is a right of war, acknowledged by the law of nations as existing in favor of one belligerent against the other, and regulated by the rules of international law.

A few extracts from an approved elementary work will be sufficient to show the nature of a blockade.

"Among the rights of belligerents, there is none more clear and incontrovertible, or more just and necessary in the application, than that which gives rise to the law of blockade. Bynkershoek says, it is founded on the principles of natural reason, as well as on the usage of nations; and Grotius considers the carrying of supplies to a besieged town, or a blockaded port, as an offence exceedingly aggravated and injurious. They both agree that a neutral may be dealt with severely; and Vattel says, he may be treated as an enemy. The law of blockade is, however, so harsh and severe in its operation, that, in order to apply it, the fact of the actual blockade must be established by clear and unequivocal evidence; and the neutral must have had due previous notice of its existence; and the squadron allotted for the purposes of its execution must be competent to cut off all communication with the interdicted place or port; and the neutral must have been guilty of some act of violation, either by going in, or attempting to enter, or by coming out with a cargo laden after the commencement of the blockade. The failure of either of the points requisite to establish the existence of a legal blockade, amounts to an entire defeasance of the measure, even though the notification of the blockade had issued from the authority of the government itself.

"A blockade must be existing in point of fact; and in order to constitute that existence, there must be a power present to enforce it."

"The definition of a blockade given by the convention of the Baltic powers, in 1780, and again in 1801, and by the ordinance of Congress, in 1781, required that there should be actually a number of vessels stationed near enough to the port to make the entry apparently dangerous."

"The occasional absence of the blockading squadron, produced by accident, as in the case of a storm, and when the station is resumed with due diligence, does not suspend the blockade, provided the suspension, and the reason of it, be known; and the law considers an attempt to take an advantage of such an accidental removal as an attempt to break the blockade, and as a mere fraud. . . . . . But if the blockade be raised by the enemy, or by applying the naval force, or a part of it, though only for a time, to other objects, or by the mere remissness of the cruisers, the commerce of neutrals to the place ought to be free. The presence of a sufficient force is the natural criterion by which the neutral is enabled to ascertain the existence of the blockade."

"The object of a blockade is not merely to prevent the importation of supplies, but to prevent export as well as import, and to cut off all communication of commerce with the blockaded port. The act of egress is as culpable as the act of ingress, if it be done fraudulently. . . . . . The modern practice does not require that the place should be invested by land as well as by sea, in order to constitute a legal blockade; and if a place be blockaded by sea only, it is no violation of belligerent rights for the neutral to carry on commerce with it by inland communications.

"It is absolutely necessary that the neutral should have had due notice of the blockade, in order to affect him with the penal consequences of a violation of it. . . . . . After the blockade is once established, and due notice received, either actually or constructively, the neutral is not permitted to go to the very station of the blockading force, under pretence of inquiring whether the blockade had terminated, because this would lead to fraudulent attempts to evade it, and would amount in practice to a universal license to attempt to enter, and, on being prevented, to claim the liberty of going elsewhere."

"A neutral cannot be permitted to place himself in the vicinity of a blockaded port, if his situation be so near that he may, with impunity, break the blockade whenever he pleases, and slip in without obstruction. If that were to be permitted, it would be impossible that any blockade could be maintained."

"The fact of clearing out or sailing for a blockaded port is, in itself, innocent, unless it be accompanied with knowledge of the blockade."

"In *Yeaton* vs. *Fry*, the Supreme Court of the United States coincided essentially with the doctrine of the English prize courts; for they held that sailing from Tobago for Curaçoa, knowing the latter to be blockaded, was a breach of the blockade, and, according to the opinion of Mr. Justice Story, in the case of the *Nereide*, 'the act of sailing with intent to break a blockade is a sufficient breach to authorize confiscation.' . . . . . If the ports be not very wide apart, the act of sailing for the blockaded port may reasonably be deemed evidence of a breach of it, and an overt act of fraud upon the belligerent rights."

" The consequence of a breach of blockade is the confiscation of the ship ; and the cargo is always, *prima facie,* implicated in the guilt of the owner or master of the ship. . . . . . If a ship has contracted guilt by a breach of blockade, the offence is not discharged until the end of the voyage. The penalty never travels on with the vessel farther than to the end of the return voyage; and if she is taken in any part of that voyage, she is taken *in delicto.*" — 1 *Kent's Com.,* 143 – 151.

It appears from all this, that a blockade admits, by implication, that the port is in the possession of a party or power with which the blockading party is at war, and with which neutral nations, if they please, may hold commercial intercourse, subject to the laws of war, without payment of duties to the party instituting the blockade, or interruption by that party except by the blockade, or other warlike operations. In other words, the port is governed for the time being, as between the blockading party and neutral nations, by the law of nations applicable to war between two powers, — instead of being governed, as to them as well as its possessors, by the domestic law applicable to the insurrectionary resistance to the established government. That government cannot say to neutrals, " We debar you from entering this port because it is blockaded, and if you violate the blockade, you will be liable to capture and condemnation," — leaving them to inquire whether the blockade is maintained, and to govern themselves by the law applicable to it, — and at the same time say, " All intercourse with the place is forbidden, because it is our port, but, by reason of insurrectionary force, commerce there cannot be carried on with the United States, and the place, therefore, is no longer to be treated as a port during the continuance of the insurrection."

4

The right to treat the insurrectionary force as a belligerent power by the institution of a blockade, thus leaving neutral nations at liberty, if they please, to hold commercial intercourse with the insurgents as a belligerent power, so far as they may without a violation of the blockade, is entirely consistent with the position that the insurgents themselves are mere rebels and traitors. In fact, any foreign nation may oblige the government assailed to resort to a blockade in order to prevent commercial intercourse with the insurgents, so far as such nation is concerned, by an acknowledgment of their independence, or, according to modern usage, by a recognition of them as a belligerent power, with a proclamation of neutrality between the contending parties, — which certainly can in no way affect the right of the existing government to deal with the insurgents as traitors, under its own municipal law. And if the government pleases to institute a blockade in anticipation of such compulsion, no implication can arise from it changing the legal relations of the parties.

Another good reason exists why the government assailed may prefer to give to the insurgent force this character of a belligerent party, so far as its relations with foreign nations are concerned. The laws of blockade, and of capture for violation of it, and the proceedings for adjudication thereupon, are, in general, well settled and defined ; while the rules which must regulate punishment for any violation of an order closing the port, and forbidding entrance into it, as a means of suppressing the insurrection, without a blockade, are not so well settled ; and attempts to deal with infractions of such order by vessels of foreign powers would lead to unnecessary collisions, certainly after a recognition of belligerency.

It has been contended that a nation cannot blockade its own ports ; but this position is not tenable when the port is in possession of a hostile force. To deny the right of blockade in such case would be to deny its right to the port, or, practically, to make it a free port until the government which formerly held and still claimed it should destroy it ; for no mere order or act for closing it could be of any avail against a foreign nation which pleased to recognize the insurgents as belligerents, without a blockade superadded.

This leads us to a more extended examination of the relations which foreign nations do or may, according to the rules of international law, sustain to those who, under the plea of Secession, are using the names and styles of several States, and who, with the assumption of State and Confederate authority, are waging insurrectionary warfare against the United States. It is apparent, from what has been said, that these relations might be either one of three different descriptions.

1. In the case of an insurrection, accompanied by an attempt to establish an independent government, a foreign nation may decline in any wise to interfere in the contest, treating the case precisely as if it were an insurrection which in no way affected its interests, except as the actual force of the insurgents interrupts the exercise of authority by the government assailed in places where that government had before exercised it, and still claims the right to continue its exercise. This is substantially the position of Russia, and, in fact, of all European and other foreign powers, as respects the United States, — Great Britain, France, and Spain excepted.

The foreign government which places itself in this relation may, and in some contingencies must, recognize the existence of the insurrection, and vary its action, or that of its citizens and subjects, accordingly. As, for instance, if the United States government should prohibit the entrance of any vessel into a particular port or ports, because the people of the place were in a state of insurrection, so that commerce with the United States under existing treaties could not be carried on there, a government declining any recognition of the insurgents, or interference with reference to the contest, would instruct its subjects, consuls, and officers to regard the prohibition, and comply with the regulation of the existing government, as if that government still possessed full jurisdiction and control over its bays, harbors, and waters, as before the existence of the insurrection, — without requiring any actual blockade of the ports in order to enforce the prohibition. It may be quite consistent with such a position for the foreign government to claim that all vessels belonging to its subjects, which should enter the ports without notice of the prohibition, should be permitted to dispose of their cargoes and depart with such clearance as could be obtained there, in the same manner as if the prohibition had not existed; because, acting in good faith toward the government, as if the insurrection did not exist, and leaving that government to contend with it without any interference or recognition of the authority or political existence of the insurgents, the foreign nation might well claim that its subjects should not suffer loss, or be prejudiced, without warning.

A foreign nation occupying such a position comes under no obligation, and owes no duty, to the insurgent power. It may carry on its commerce with the government assailed without any liability, under the law of nations, to search and seizure for contraband goods. It may avail itself of any implied recognition of the insurgents by the government assailed, as by the institution of a blockade, and insist that its subjects have a right to hold commercial intercourse with the insurrectionary power as a belligerent, so far as they may consistently with the blockade. It will naturally refuse to permit its vessels to be overhauled and detained by vessels commissioned by the insurgents as privateers, and may well treat such interference as piratical; although it will be at its pleasure, and consistent with its position, to permit such visitation as may serve to ascertain the nationality of its vessels, without any search for enemies' property, or articles contraband of war.

Such a position would by no means require the foreign nation, which ignored the insurgent force as an existing power, to treat the privateers commissioned by the insurrectionary government as pirates. It is true, that the British government, in the case of Greece, in 1825, alleged that " a power or a community which was at war with another, and which covered the sea with its cruisers, must either be acknowledged as a belligerent, or dealt with as a pirate." But the necessity is certainly not apparent, in respect to any nation whose vessels are not interfered with by such cruisers. With the exception of nations whose commerce is assailed, it is not necessarily an objection to a privateer that she holds a commission from an unrecognized power. Piracy, it is evident, may be of a general, or of a limited character. The slave-trade is piracy under the laws of Great Britain and of the United States. But this does not constitute it piracy as to other nations. And the same may be true of that description of piracy which consists in robbing merchant-vessels on the high seas. The fact, that those who act as privateers under commissions from the Confederate States are pirates by the express provision of the act of Congress before cited, as regards the United States, against whose vessels they direct their warfare, does not constitute them pirates as respects other nations. And the result would be the same, if, by the rules of public law, also, the United States might hold them to be pirates. France, before her recognition of the independence of the United American Colonies, did not treat their privateers as pirates; and the government of the United States has in several instances acted on the principle that privateers of insurgents not acknowledged were not pirates as to the United States, and were not subject to capture as such.* But if a vessel commissioned as a privateer by an unrecognized belligerent rob a vessel of a neutral nation, may not any nation treat the act as piracy? †

2. Any foreign nation, whenever the circumstances are such as to warrant it, may acknowledge, for itself, the independence

---

* 3 Wheaton's Reports, 610, United States *vs.* Palmer; 7 Wheaton's Rep. 283, The Santissima Trinidad; Case of Captain P. P. Voorhies, before a naval court-martial, in 1844.

† 1 Phillimore's Int. Law, 398 – 406.

of an insurgent organization, recognizing it as having a national existence, and treating it as a nation ; in which case it may form an alliance with the insurgent government, offensive and defensive; and thus become a party to the war ; or it may, with such acknowledgment, assume a position of neutrality, claiming the rights of a neutral, as between what would then, to the party recognizing the independence of the insurgents, be two equally independent belligerent nations. Such acknowledgment of the independence of an insurgent party, before its independence is recognized by the government which it assails, may or may not furnish just cause of war on the part of that government, according to the circumstances under which it is made. If the acknowledgment follows very soon upon the breaking out of the insurrection, and while the government is pursuing active and energetic measures to suppress it, the aid and encouragement thereby given to the rebels would furnish just cause of offence to the existing government. On the other hand, after the contest has been of long continuance, and the independence of the insurrectionary party has been practically maintained for such a period as to show its capacity to uphold it, then the interests of other nations may well justify them in an acknowledgment of what has been accomplished, — in a recognition of an existing fact, — without just cause of offence to the government which has been resisted, and which has failed to overcome that resistance. The commercial interests of nations having no interest in the contest may require that they should make the recognition, for the purpose of trade, or for other desirable ends ; and the existing government cannot complain of the mere acknowledgment of an actual fact. But such recognition should follow only a practical independence. Such was the case with the acknowledgment of the independence of the South American republics by the United States in 1823, the latter assuming to act as a neutral nation.

The insurgent party, upon such acknowledgment, may

claim the right to send an ambassador or minister to the nation making it, and may expect in due course of time to receive one, and to have their intercourse regulated by treaty. After such an acknowledgment, if the nation making it does not become a party to the war, — either by a treaty of alliance with the party thus recognized, or by a declaration of war by the government assailed, on account of the recognition, — the nation making the acknowledgment is entitled to claim the rights of a neutral with respect to each of the belligerent parties, treating each as a nation, and forming treaties with the insurgent party, as if it were a nation, equally with its adversary; and it may send and receive ambassadors, and trade to and from any ports occupied and held by the party acknowledged, except so far as it is prevented by the exercise of rights accorded by international law to belligerents against neutrals.

The neutral nation has the right to require that its territory shall not be made the theatre of war, nor made use of for the purposes of war, and that hostile enterprises shall not originate in, or be carried on, from it. Its citizens and subjects may be the carriers of the goods of either belligerent, subject to the right of the other belligerent to capture such goods, and to search and detain the neutral vessel for that purpose, but not to confiscate the ship; and they may maintain free commercial intercourse with each belligerent, subject to the rules which forbid aid to the belligerent in the prosecution of the war, and to the right of the belligerent to prevent such intercourse by an efficient blockade.

The duty of the neutral is not to favor one belligerent to the detriment of the other, — not to transport munitions of war, or other goods contraband of war, to either belligerent, — not to carry officers, soldiers, or despatches of either, — to respect any blockade by one belligerent, of the ports of the other, if it is efficient, — and, generally, not to aid either belligerent, in the prosecution of the war, except as the ordinary commercial transactions in goods not contraband incidentally furnish such aid.

The rights of the belligerent as respects the neutral are, to visit and search his merchant-vessels, on the high seas, for the purpose of ascertaining whether enemies' property, or goods contraband of war, or persons whom the neutral may not carry, are on board ; to capture the property of the enemy so found ;* and for violation of belligerent rights, by aid rendered to the enemy in transporting goods contraband of war, or persons in the service of the enemy in the prosecution of the war, as officers, soldiers, or other functionaries, or the despatches of the enemy, — and also for violation of blockade, — to capture and confiscate the ship and goods.

These are the principal rights and duties of the parties, as set forth, in substance, by accredited writers on international law, subject in some instances to limitations and modifications, to which we shall refer, so far as they appear to be material to the present discussion.

No nation has as yet acknowledged the independence of the Confederate States. Such acknowledgment is not usually made, unless by a nation which is disposed to ally itself with the insurgents in hostility to the government assailed, until the independence of the insurgents has been acknowledged by that government, or until it has been practically achieved.

3. It is competent for any foreign nation, from the time when an insurrectionary force assumes to institute a form of government, and to carry on a war, to recognize the insurgents as a belligerent party.

Considerations of policy, as well as of comity, may well postpone such a recognition until there has been ample time for the government assailed to assert its power for the suppression of the insurrection. But these are matters of which each nation must judge for itself. Great Britain was the first to make such recognition of the Confederate States. France and Spain have since followed the example.

---

* See Appendix, Note A.

In one sense, this is but the recognition of an existing fact. It seems, however, to carry with it something more than a mere acknowledgment of the fact that there is a state of civil war existing; for that fact may be recognized, spoken of, deplored, and sympathy expressed, as has been done by Russia, without any political consequences attached to such recognition.

The formal recognition of the insurgent party as a belligerent, by another nation, gives the insurgents a political *status* as to the party making the recognition, and involves consequences to the government which is attempting to suppress the insurrection, as has been already suggested. This recognition appears to be an action intermediate as regards the other two, and to be a convenient mode of dealing with a case of intestine war by a foreign nation which is desirous of being civil to the insurgent party, and of availing itself of all the intercourse which can be established with them, without committing itself to an acknowledgment of an independence which may never be achieved, and without the establishment of diplomatic relations, which might be suddenly terminated, and in a manner not greatly to the credit of the neutral, making the acknowledgment of an independence which was proved to be an abortion by the suppression of the rebellion very soon afterward.

As Great Britain was the first to acknowledge the belligerency of the Confederates, and as this acknowledgment is the only one which has affected the relations of the United States in any considerable degree, we shall pursue the residue of our discussion with a more particular reference to the existing relations between Great Britain and the United States. Her acknowledgment did not give the insurgents a right to send an ambassador to the Court of St. James, nor to claim a treaty of amity and commercial relations. It did not place them, as respects her, in the position of a nation. But, being acquiesced in by the United States, it gave her rights as against them which she could not have had, as a neutral nation, but for the recognition; and it also operated to give rights to the insurgent government as against her, which she would not otherwise have permitted it to enjoy.

Great Britain declared that she was cognizant of the fact that a civil war existed in the·United States. That is nothing. All the rest of the civilized world knew the same thing. But by adding the recognition, she accorded to them the warlike rights of a belligerent nation ; and by her superadded declaration of strict neutrality, she allowed to them, for the general purposes of commercial intercourse and warlike operations, all the rights which she allows to the United States, aside from previous treaty stipulations. She bound herself to respect their "stars and bars" equally with the flag of the United States. If, in her existing treaty with the United States, there are any stipulations on her part, the performance of which would conflict with the recognition which she thus made, and the neutrality which she thus assumed, the question might arise, between her and the Confederates, how far she had a right, under the law of nations, to perform those stipulations without a breach of her neutrality. She knew that, at the date of her present treaty with the United States, all the ports in the seceding States, so called, were in the possession of the general government, and that the duties there paid were part of the common funds of the whole United States. She knew that at the time of her recognition those ports were in the possession of the insurgents, who claimed to regulate the commercial intercourse there, and to appropriate the revenues derived therefrom to other uses than to those of the United States. And she knew also how the revenue of the United States would be injuriously affected, by the facilities for smuggling into the Northern States goods introduced through those ports, if a free commerce were carried on there. Yet, by her recognition of the Confederate States as an existing power, she acknowledges those ports to be the ports of the party in possession, and claims the right, as a neutral nation, to enter those ports, and any others which may be opened by the Confederate States, with her ships and goods, unless the United States government shall enforce its attempts to suppress the insurrection there by an efficient blockade, precisely as she would be authorized to do in the case of two long existing independent nations contending in war, and to which she held the relation of neutrality. The United States are attempting to keep up such a blockade.

It is true that the United States were not compelled to resort to the blockade by reason of her recognition. The intention to blockade was proclaimed on the 19th of April, which was before the recognition. But it is also true, we think, that that recognition, which was in May,* was in no manner influenced by the implied recognition arising from the blockade. Her recognition of the insurgents as a belligerent party has therefore, to this extent, by her voluntary act, given them the standing of a nation, although there is no acknowledgment of their independence. The blockade itself would not necessarily have done this; and but for the recognition, it might have been terminated at pleasure, so far as Great Britain was concerned, and any other measure of coercion have been substituted.

It has been said, without much consideration, that British ships would have had a right to resort to those ports without

---

* There has been an attempt to controvert the position in the article on "Habeas Corpus and Martial Law " in our last number, that Mr. Chief Justice Taney ought, in Merryman's case, to have taken notice of the existence of the war. The position itself is of very little importance to the argument, — which was to show that the refusal of General Cadwalader to produce his prisoner was sustained by sound principles; for the Chief Justice very plainly intimated that, if General Cadwalader had himself undertaken to suspend the *habeas corpus*, (in other words, to deny his liability to bring in his prisoner,) he would not have taken the trouble to argue the question. But it appears that the Lord Chancellor and other legal authorities in England had found out that war existed here some time before Merryman's case came before the Chief Justice, which was on the 28th day of May. And as the information respecting the facts which served to show its existence was not confined exclusively to that country, perhaps, if Mr. Chief Justice Taney had inquired, he might have found it out also.

any such recognition, if there was not an actual blockade, because, the right of secession being denied by the United States, they are still ports of entry under the laws of the United States, the President having no power to repeal the laws constituting them ports of entry. It is readily conceded that the President has no power to repeal a law ; but we have already suggested that he might, by reason of the insurrection, which prevented the collection of the duties, and for the purpose of suppressing that insurrection, close the ports by a proclamation, which all foreign nations that did not recognize the belligerent *status* of the Confederate States would be bound to respect. If there was in fact a doubt respecting his constitutional power, the intercourse of foreign nations with the United States is through the Executive, and they are not authorized to go behind his acts, and to allege that they are nugatory, because under the provisions of the Constitution a power which he attempts to exercise is vested only in Congress.* There is no need, however, of saying this in a curt or spicy manner.

Moreover, without regard to any question of right legally to close the ports, foreign nations could not claim to enter those ports, as ports of the United States, after they had been notified by the Executive that they could not make their entries there under the authority of the United States, — that duties paid there would be paid to insurgents, — and that clearances there must be taken from parties at war with the United States ; for which reason, and for the suppression of the insurrection, entries were forbidden.

But the burden of the recognition seems not to be altogether upon the United States. Great Britain appears there-

---

* Mr. Jefferson Davis understands this. In his first message to the Confederate Congress, he said that the proclamation of President Lincoln was a plain declaration of war, which he was not at liberty to disregard, because of his knowledge that, under the Constitution, the President was usurping a power granted exclusively to Congress. "He is the sole organ of communication between that country and foreign powers."

by to have subjected her merchant-vessels not only to a right of visit to ascertain their nationality, but to a right of search and capture, in the same manner, and to the same extent, as she would have done had she acknowledged their independence. If the United States must accord to her the rights of a neutral nation, by an efficient blockade, in order to exclude her vessels from the Southern ports, they must certainly have the rights of a belligerent against a neutral, and may capture, in her merchant-ships, goods the property of the enemy, all articles known as contraband of war, and all persons whose carriage by the neutral is not in strict accordance with the neutrality.

The privateers commissioned by Mr. Jefferson Davis may, in like manner, search British merchant-vessels with similar rights, and for any abuse of the power her reclamation for damages is upon " King Cotton," if he is not in the mean time consumed by his own or some other fires.

Whether the Confederate privateers will also be authorized to capture such loyal citizens of the States which have seceded as may be found on board of British vessels, — but having no military or hostile character except as they are citizens of the United States, — and turn them over to the Confederate government as prisoners at twenty-five dollars per head, according to the tenor of the law under which they are commissioned, is perhaps not so clear. Upon the principle, or want of principle, of what the London Times now calls the " antiquated law," by which Great Britain claimed a right to search, and take her subjects from, the vessels of the United States, she would be bound to admit the right of the United States to take their citizens from her vessels ; and giving equal rights to the Confederate States, the question would arise whether all citizens of the seceded States are included within the rule. This assumption of burdens, however, is her affair, not ours. We merely advert to it as one of the incidents which attends the recognition.

It seems very apparent, from what we have stated, that the recognition of the Confederate States as a belligerent power has substantially the effect of an acknowledgment of their independence, except that it does not authorize a demand of diplomatic intercourse and the formation of treaties. How far was such an early recognition justified by history?

The long civil war of her South American Colonies against Spain, and their establishment of independent governments *de facto*, required a recognition of them by the United States. Lord John Russell referred to the recognition of Greece, in her war against Turkey, as furnishing a precedent. We are not advised that he referred to any other. But the precedent fails entirely, except as to the fact of that kind of recognition. Greece had no share nor voice in the government of herself, still less in governing Turkey at the same time. She had not furnished three quarters of the Sultans who within less than a century had occupied the throne at Constantinople, and she had not, by one enginery or another, shaped the legislation of the great divan of the Turkish empire so as to suit her purposes, in three quarters of the political measures adopted there during the same time. No state had been annexed to the empire for her aggrandizement, and to give her political strength; and no war had been waged for the acquisition of Mexican or other territory in order that she might diffuse through it her peculiar institutions. On the contrary, she had been subjugated, though not entirely conquered; subdued, with the exception of the almost wild inhabitants of her mountain fastnesses; and ground into the dust by the iron heel of a military oppression which spared neither age nor sex, — which wrested from labor the reward of its toil, and snatched from hunger the morsel necessary to save it from becoming starvation.

This people rose up in their might against their oppressors, in 1821, reasserting their national existence; and after a warfare of more than four years, — a warfare of immeasurable atrocity on the part of the Turks, and almost corresponding ferocity on the part of the Greeks, — a warfare which placed Missolonghi and Navarino on the page of history by the side of Marathon, and immortalized, among many others, the names of Mavrocordato, Colettis, Kanaris, Botzaris, and Miaulis, — the British government issued " a decided declaration of neutrality " between the belligerents.

The conclusion seems to follow, that the acknowledgment of a belligerent *status* of the Confederation, before the administration of President Lincoln had had time to determine upon its measures and organize its forces for the suppression of the insurrection, — with the attempt to carry on a neutral commerce with the ports within its limits, which ports are *de jure* still within the United States and under the jurisdiction of that government, and were only *de facto* without their jurisdiction, by the force of an insurrection of from four to six months' duration, — is entirely without a precedent, and might well be deemed a grave ground of offence to the United States, had not the blockade been previously instituted. It has undoubtedly been the cause of deep feeling among the people. We are aware that Dr. Phillimore says: " There is no proposition of law upon which there exists a more universal agreement of all jurists than upon this; viz. that this virtual and *de facto* recognition of a new state gives no just cause of offence to the old state, inasmuch as it decides nothing concerning the asserted rights of the latter. For if they be eventually sustained and made triumphant, they cannot be questioned by the third power, which, pending the conflict, has virtually recognized the revolted state." *   But he is speaking of such recognitions as were made by Great Britain of the South American Colonies, after a struggle between them and Spain of about twelve years; and he refers to President Monroe's message of December, 1823, and to the speeches of Mr. Canning and Sir

---

* 2 Phill. on International Law, 18.

James Mackintosh upon that subject, as his authorities for the proposition.

A recognition following soon after the breaking out of an insurrection, and where from the peculiar circumstances there are special difficulties in organizing the forces of the government for the suppression of it, has the effect of giving an encouragement to it, which a nation in amity with the existing government, and desirous of continuing that relation, is not authorized to give.

The British government were as little prepared for the breaking out of the insurrection in India as the United States were for that of the South; but the arm of the government was not paralyzed, for the time, by a complicity of Cabinet officers with the insurrection, and by such a state of inaction, if not complicity, on the part of the head of the administration, that nothing effective could be accomplished to arrest it until the traitors of the Cabinet had been forced to send in their unwilling resignations. Besides, the available military force of the British near the scene of warlike operations was much more readily concentrated, and comparatively of much greater efficiency, than that of the United States; and (excepting native troops) it had few or no traitors in it. Still, with all these advantages, the British power in India was for a considerable period shaken to its foundation, and it was said in high quarters that "India was to be reconquered." Now suppose that, at about the time when Havelock began to move effectively for the suppression of the rebellion, some member of Congress had arisen in his place, and proposed a formal acknowledgment of the independence of British India. That would have been but the act of an individual legislator, who, not being the authorized exponent of the views of the administration, could in no wise compromise the government itself. But suppose the authorized Cabinet officials had thereupon, if not in hot haste, yet under no circumstances of necessity, proceeded to declare that the United States had concluded to recognize the king of

Delhi and his adherents as belligerents. The English government would undoubtedly have regarded this as an evidence of hostility, not entirely rebutted by any proclamation of strict neutrality which might have accompanied it. Yet such a proceeding would not have given courage and confidence to his Majesty of Delhi and his confederates to persevere in their rebellion.

Such are some of the relations of the United States, domestic and foreign, arising from the insurrection in the Southern States, as they exist at the present time. What are the reasonable speculations for the future on this subject?

The Confederate War Secretary, upon the occasion of the bombardment of Fort Sumter, prophesied that the Confederate flag would float over the dome of the old Capitol before the first of May; and he added: "Let them try Southern chivalry, and test the extent of Southern resources, and it might float eventually over Faneuil Hall itself." Well, Southern chivalry has been tried. It began by stealing all the public property it could lay its hands on, and then issuing letters of marque and reprisal before a particle of property had been taken by the United States, or any injury had been done to the Confederacy which could by any possible construction warrant *reprisals*. It has proceeded by the confiscation of the property of those who, having faith in the securities of Southern States and Southern people, had invested in such State securities, or given credit to traders for merchandise; and this without regard to any act done by such holders of stocks or creditors, but merely because certain people of the Southern States chose to rebel against the government of the United States, that government resisted the attempt, and the stockholders and creditors were, ever had been, and still remained citizens of the United States. Chivalry finds its only justification for this seizure of private property in the fact, that the government under which all the parties have heretofore lived, and to which all acknowledged a common allegiance, resists the efforts of the debtors to accomplish a revolution. Chivalry has been tested in arms, as well as in legislation, and it manifests itself in masked batteries and ambuscades, the hoisting of false flags and signals, and all manner of false pretences for the purpose of securing an unequal advantage. Chivalry thus far is cooped up within the limits of the States seceding, except that, in violation of all its State-rights theory, it is insisting that Missouri and Kentucky, against the expressed will of the people of those States, shall join in the rebellion ; and it has thereupon attempted to overrun the former, and has made a lodgement in the southern portion of the latter. As an offset to this, it has lost Western Virginia, considerable portions of the eastern part of that State, and several positions on the seaboard in other States. It stands now, and, so far as at present can be judged, it is likely to stand, very much on the defensive, unless Southern "resources" come to the rescue.

Thus far Southern resources have not shown to much better advantage than Southern chivalry. Proposals for a loan of fifteen millions of dollars are said to have realized ten millions. A project for a loan of cotton to the amount of one hundred millions is admitted to be a failure, because the "king" is shut up on a barren throne within his dominions, and cannot there be made negotiable. A tax of fifteen millions remains to be collected in such manner as it may be. In the mean time an issue of one hundred millions of Confederate bonds has no convertibility into coin, and no basis of redemption, and can therefore have no credit outside the limits of the Confederacy, and none within it except such as is enforced by the necessities of the war. Banks have suspended specie payments, and coin of all descriptions is at an extravagant premium. External trade is nearly all cut off by means of the blockade, a few arrivals and clearances, through a surreptitious evasion of it, furnishing only an exceedingly limited supply of munitions of war and foreign goods. Of manufacturing and domestic trade there can, under these circumstances, be but a very small amount, except in connection with supplies for the army ; and many descriptions of what are ordinarily regarded as the necessaries of life are, in particular districts, at almost famine prices. On the other hand, the agricultural crops for the present year are supposed to have been abundant, so that there is no prospect of the termination of the war by absolute starvation.

In discussing the question of the probable duration of the war, it has been suggested that the people of the South are fighting, or, what is the same thing, believe they are fighting, for their liberties ; and that, in all controversies of such a character, there is a pertinacity of purpose, which continues the contest without resources, and under all deprivations and reverses, until a final victory is achieved. One of the resources of the leaders of the rebellion has been the representation to the great mass of their misguided followers, that this is a war of subjugation, and that, if they fail to fight to the last extremity, their liberties will be lost. But the sober second-thought, if that thought ever comes, will show them that the termination of the war will leave the several States which have attempted to secede in the possession of all their rights of sovereignty, and in all the control of their municipal affairs which they have ever had since the adoption of the Constitution, — except so far as the rebellion has introduced revolution into any particular State, through which some of them may possibly find themselves dismembered by the action of their own people, — and except as the situation and legal condition of their slaves may, to a very material extent, be changed, if the war is protracted.

That the war must continue on the part of the North until the navigation of the Mississippi, from its sources to its mouth, is secured to the people of the Northwest, so that no hostile power upon its banks can impede such navigation, or until the Northern States are rendered powerless to prosecute the contest to a successful issue, may be assumed to be certain. The promptitude with which batteries were erected on the banks of that river immediately after the outburst of the secession, for the purpose of controlling and closing the navigation of it, and thereby coercing the people of the Northwestern States into submission to the rebel power, shows conclusively that there can be no security for the free navigation of it except by holding it, and its banks on either side, within the jurisdiction of the United States. The great facilities for smuggling, through the entry of goods into the Southern ports and their subsequent introduction into the North along such an extensive line of inland frontier as would exist on a separation of the States, — and the fact that rival interests would create sources of constant irritation, — furnish other reasons why the eventual establishment of the authority of the United States must be sought by the Northern States, even through a protracted contest, and at an enormous sacrifice. With victory secured, the North would rise up with renewed energy, and with its own material interests comparatively unimpaired, except by a decrease in the demand for articles heretofore furnished to the South.

Not so with the South. With a protracted contest, even victory is a substantial defeat. Cotton, which has been supposed to be the great resource to carry them through the revolution, has, as we have seen, thus far proved a failure. It cannot be applied as a means to carry on the war to any great extent, except by a conversion into money or other articles; and as this could not be effected, the crop of the present year remains on hand. Only a certain amount of cotton, more or less, is required for the consumption of the world, and this crop, if it could have found a market, would have supplied the demand in England, France, and the Northern States. With the diminished demand for manufactured articles, the supply from other quarters has thus far sufficed, so that no great distress has supervened from the want of Southern cotton; not more, probably, than ordinarily occurs in the course of a commercial revulsion, perhaps not so much. Another full crop, if raised before this is disposed of, will operate as a reduction of its ordinary value, by furnishing an excess of supply for the existing machinery. In the mean time, every year's delay in getting it to market stimulates the cultivation of cotton abroad. If the present state of things continues two or three years, the competition of foreign cotton will reduce the price to perhaps two thirds, or even one half, of the rate heretofore paid; and with this reduction comes a corresponding reduction in the value of slaves and the value of plantations. It is for the interest of Great Britain to foster and protect the growth of cotton in her own dominions, and the production of a sufficient amount within her territory once secured, American cotton will not be allowed to ruin that source of national wealth.

Another resource of the South, which has thus far been the means of strength in the prosecution of the war, is slavery. The slaves are the producers, and the masters can all the better be spared to fill the ranks of the army. It will continue to be so until the troops of the United States penetrate the slave territory. Until that time, proclamations for emancipation, from whatever source, will be of no avail. The President and Congress have no more authority to emancipate the slaves, than the writer of this article. An attempt so to do would be a gross usurpation of power. The general at the head of the army has no right to emancipate them, except as an incident to military occupations and operations; and whatever theory may exist on that subject, he can accomplish nothing further than he penetrates the country. So far as he does this, the question of his right to issue a proclamation for that purpose is not very material. The emancipation will take care for itself. He cannot fight the rebels successfully, and at the same time aid them to hold their slaves; and the result is practical freedom. If they avail themselves of it, because their masters have escaped from them, then there is no fugitive slave law to return them after the rebellion is suppressed. But if they remain until their masters have resumed their occupation under State authority on the return of peace, this practical freedom is not likely to prevent their return to bondage. When, however, the Northern army has made a successful march through Virginia into South Carolina, there is another result, which, while it cannot be contemplated but with horror, must, if it occur, be charged to those whose madness will have brought it upon them.

The great resource upon which the South has relied to carry it successfully through a revolution, has been the interference of Great Britain and France. It was assumed that cotton was a king at whose feet the people of Europe must prostrate themselves and their principles, and that, if Southern chivalry could not fight its own battles, they would, through this instrumentality, be fought for it by other powers. It remains to be seen whether this resource will be made available to the accomplishment of the object. What is the probability of such interference?

Without assuming the office of a prophet, we venture to express a confident belief that there will be no immediate change in the relations which at present exist between the United States and foreign powers, unless some new, and at present improbable, complication of those relations shall give rise to new and grave causes of hostility.

The sympathy of Russia with the United States has been manifested in a most friendly and generous manner.

Spain, not only in her proclamation of neutrality, but in the enforcement of it by the release of the prizes sent into Cienfuegos by the privateer Sumter, has given conclusive evidence that she has no sympathy with the rebellion.

With respect to France, there has been no supposition that there was danger of collision. The course thus far pursued by Napoleon III., and by the people of the French empire, while it has evinced a deep solicitude respecting the effect which the civil war might have upon the material interests of France, has at the same time furnished satisfactory evidence that the French government and the French people — with some exceptions certainly among their press and people — are disposed to accord to the United States all their rights, upon the most fair interpretation of the law of nations.

What is the probability that Great Britain will belie all her professions in favor of free principles, and tarnish her fair fame by an alliance with a rebellion, which, caused almost entirely by the opposition of the North to the extension of slavery, has organized a Confederacy with slavery for its chief corner-stone, and which, if successful in establishing its independence, will soon insist upon opening the slave-trade ?

There are certainly no grave causes of controversy or hostility between the United States and Great Britain. More than two generations of mankind have passed away since the period of the American Revolution, and very few remain within the confines of this world whose fading memories retain even a faint remembrance of that contest. The controversies which led to the war of 1812 have either been amicably settled, or have fallen out of sight, and there can be no rankling bitterness which arose out of them still remaining to find expression in the promotion of another war. Most of those who, on either side, were actively engaged in that contest, have laid their hostility to rest in the bosom of their common mother, — earth. That all causes of difference arising from two wars, and from divers controversies respecting boundaries, and other matters of dispute, had left no evil feeling on the part of the people of the United States, or at least the Northern and Western portion of them, was made most clearly apparent upon the occasion of the visit of the Prince of Wales to this country in 1860. There could not possibly be a more exuberant manifestation of perfect friendship than was exhibited, not only by all persons in official station, but by the great masses of the people, of all classes and conditions, from the time when the heir apparent set his foot upon the soil of Michigan, until the moment when it left its last imprint upon that of Maine on his departure homeward. If there was any one who was weak enough to suppose that the grand pageant, which continued almost without interruption from day to day during his progress through the country, — in which President and Cabinet, governors and judges, senators and representatives, vied with one another in proffers of respect and courtesy, and in which the great body of the people made the welkin ring with their shouts of welcome, — was a mere demonstration of joy at the sight of a live prince, or a weak cringing to royalty, he must have greatly misunderstood the signs of the times. The enthusiasm, which seemed almost unbounded, while it was undoubtedly a spontaneous testimonial of respect to the Queen, showing the popular estimation of her Majesty as a sovereign, a woman, a wife, and a mother, was at the same time a demonstration of gushing good feeling for the government of the country and its people at large. Old causes of feud were forgotten, — rival industrial interests were for the time but as matters for a generous competition, — taunting words, which in bygone days had been profusely dispensed, gave place to courteous speech, which not only came trippingly from the tongue, but which welled up from the heart.

There was certainly no little cause for astonishment, and there might well be no little revulsion of feeling, on the part of the people of the Northern States, when, within some six months afterward, and before the incoming administration had time to make preparations for suppressing the insurrection, there was an effort in Parliament to give strength to it, by an acknowledgment of the independence of the Confederacy, and the establishment of commercial relations with it, which found large countenance from the English press.

It may be admitted — it is undoubtedly true — that much of this offensive demonstration had its origin, not in feelings of hostility, but in a belief that the rebellion must succeed, and in anticipated commercial relations with the new-born power thus proposed to be baptized into the great national and commercial church universal; which was — even upon the supposition of its existence — the offspring of treason and fraud, lying in a cradle constructed by theft and robbery, and rocked and nursed by African slavery. But it appeared somewhat remarkable that the wise politicians who were thus willing to overlook the stigma upon the parentage of the bantling for which they were ready to stand as political godfathers, should at the same time have ignored the fact that the commercial intercourse of the Northern States was of some value to Great Britain, and that this was likely to be seriously interrupted at no distant day, if their project was accomplished. It may be, however, that they supposed, with the London Economist, that the dismemberment of the Union would paralyze both sections. The Economist, while disclaiming "any feeling of hostility, very frankly admitted its joy at the prospect of the dismemberment, not merely on account of the commercial advantages to accrue to England, but because it would destroy the power of the people of the United States, and put an end to their vain boasting. As for the "boasting," it is quite true that in speeches in Congress, in inflammatory editorials, in fourth of July orations, lyceum lectures, and sometimes in things called sermons, we exhibit enough, and more than enough, of that miserable spirit; no small portion of it being (if regarded at all) offensive to England and Englishmen, although it is specially designed for home consumption. But there are at least two things to be considered in extenuation. We know what people, of all the world, have heretofore set us the example in this respect; and we know also from what people in bygone and later days have come the taunts and the disparagement which have given rise to no small portion of it. But when we gave the Prince of Wales his great ovation, we were not thinking of the old

inquiry, " Who reads an American book ? " nor of the char-
acteristics which have more recently, over the water, been
assigned to " our American cousins " and their democratic
government. Whatever may have been said by politicians in
Congress or out of Congress, or by newspaper correspondents
or editors, or in great and small orations, furnishes no good
reason why Great Britain should interfere on the Confederate
side, in this civil war. A full share of this offensive boasting
has had its location south of Mason and Dixon's line.

It was for a long time expected by the Southern leaders
that Great Britain would raise the blockade to procure a supply of cotton, and great efforts were made to represent that it
was not efficient. We had been at some pains to procure sta-
tistics on which to base a trustworthy estimate of the supply of
cotton which will be received in Great Britain in 1862 from
other sources than the Southern States, for the purpose of
showing that her necessities in this respect would furnish no
excuse for any such interference. No evil, such as ordinarily attends a commercial crisis, could furnish a sufficient
reason. But we are relieved from a discussion of this subject
by the London Economist, which — referring to the notion of
the Southern political leaders, " that by starving France and
England, by the loss and suffering anticipated as the consequences of an entire privation of the American cotton supply, they will compel those governments to interfere on their
behalf, and force the United States to abandon the blockade "
— says : —

" If they really expect such a high-handed violation of all international usage on our part, we can only say their leaders are less sen-
sible and experienced men than we have hitherto supposed. There is
not the remotest chance that either power would feel justified for a
moment in projecting such an act of decided and unwarrantable hostility against the United States. We are less dependent upon the South
than the South is upon us, as they will erelong begin to discover. It
is more necessary for them to sell, than for us to buy. As we have

more than once shown, the worst that can happen to us from a continuance of the blockade will be, that our mills will have to work two-thirds time; and it is by no means sure from present appearances whether the aggregate demand of the world would suffice to take off much more than three fourths of a full production, even if we had cotton in abundance."

The allegation that the blockade has not been so far effective as to comply with the rules of international law on that subject, if it may have been true at some places, has not been so to the extent which has been represented. The blockading force has in most instances been sufficient to make any open attempt to enter or leave the port dangerous. The number of arrivals and departures, which has been paraded as evidence of its inefficiency, furnishes no proof against it. Nearly all of them have been fraudulent evasions of the blockade.

It is not incumbent on the party instituting a blockade to station a force at all the inlets and petty harbors on the coast, where there is no recognized port; where no entry could be made, or clearance had, in time of peace; and where, of course, if any commerce were carried on, it would be smuggling, and not a lawful commerce. Any running into and out of such places, in order to avoid the danger of the blockading force, is fraudulent, and has no tendency to show that the blockade is not effective.

Nor is it necessary that the blockading force should be such that a vessel, taking advantage of a skilful pilot and the darkness of midnight, cannot make her entry, or exit, without being discovered. To require such a blockade would be to require an impracticability. Vessels navigated by steam, to say nothing of sailing-vessels, by selecting their time, can in many instances run a blockade.

Whether the contrivances to evade the blockade are by the petty codfish hucksters of the Anglo-American colonies, who fraudulently clear for some of the West India Islands, and then slyly slip into Hatteras or some other inlet; or whether by the more pretentious "greedy merchants" of Hartlepool or some other "pool" on the English coast, "who care not how things go, provided they can but satisfy their thirst of gain,"[*] and who, violating at the same time the laws of their own government and those of the United States, the vaunted principles of British freedom and the proprieties of national intercommunication, sneak, in the darkness of night, into the harbor of Savannah or of Charleston, for the sake of acquiring the "almighty dollar" with the love of which they delight to taunt the Yankees; — it does not rest with Great Britain to allege that the success of such attempts, however numerous, by those whom she must admit to be, thus far, her unworthy subjects, can show an insufficiency of the blockade.

Almost at the time when we were writing the last sentence, the foreign relations of the United States were further complicated by the seizure of Messrs. Mason and Slidell, on board the British steamer Trent, on her passage from Havana to St. Thomas, she being at the time on the high seas, and being (it is understood) a passenger vessel, owned by private parties, but carrying the British and foreign mails by contract with the government.

Messrs. Mason and Slidell had recently left the port of Charleston, in a vessel belonging to parties there, for the purpose of proceeding to Europe, by way of Havana, as "Ambassadors of the Confederate States," as they have generally been called; but a more correct designation would be, as the agents or commissioners of the Confederate government, for the purpose, it may be presumed from other facts too numerous here to be stated, of obtaining, if possible, an acknowledgment of the independence of the Confederate States, — of communicating with their agents already there, — and of aiding in the adoption of such measures as might promote the interests of those States in the existing war with the United States, by ne-

---

* Puffendorff, cited by Sir William Scott, 1 Rob. Adm. Rep. 352.

gotiations for the purchase of arms and munitions of war, and their transportation to the ports of the Southern States. ·

Mr. Jefferson Davis, in his late message to the Confederate Congress, speaks of them as " the distinguished gentlemen whom, with your approval, at the last session, I commissioned to represent the Confederacy at certain foreign courts "; and he charges the United States with having " violated the rights of embassy, for the most part held sacred even among barbarians, by seizing our ministers whilst under the protection and within the dominions of a neutral nation." It may be noted that this shows conclusively that their original destination was Europe, — that their proceeding to Havana in the first instance was merely for security, or convenience, and transshipment, — and thus that their voyage on board the Trent was merely a continuation of a voyage from Charleston to Europe. They were bearers of despatches, also, of the character of which we shall speak hereafter.

From this designation of them as "Ministers" and "Ambassadors," in the message, and elsewhere, it was but a matter of course that much of the discussion, in the papers of the day, has been upon the question of the right of a belligerent to stop the *ambassador* of his enemy. The right is asserted by Vattel. It is reasserted by Sir William Scott, in this language: —

"I have before said, that persons discharging the functions of ambassadors are, in a peculiar manner, objects of the protection and favor of the law of nations. The limits that are assigned to the operations of war against *them*, by *Vattel*, and other writers upon those subjects, are, that you may exercise your right of *war against them*, wherever the character of hostility exists. *You may stop the ambassador of your enemy on his passage;* but when he has arrived, and has taken upon himself the functions of his office, and has been admitted in his representative character, he becomes a sort of *middle*-man, entitled to peculiar *privileges*, as set apart for the protection of the relations of amity and peace, in maintaining which all nations are in some degree interested."— *Case of the Caroline,* 6 Robinson's Adm. Rep. 467, 468.

The doctrine thus stated may, as between England and the United States, be regarded as a sound principle of international law.

" You may stop the ambassador of your enemy on his passage " ? When, and where, and on what passage, may you stop him ? It has been argued, in reference to this case, in substance, that he may be stopped only while in his own country, or while passing through the country with which his government is at war, or on the high seas in a vessel of his own country ; and that in this case the stoppage was unlawful, because the ambassador when in a neutral vessel is in a neutral territory. Mr. Jefferson Davis falls into this error. He speaks, as appears in the extract above quoted, of seizing " our ministers while under the protection and within the dominions of a neutral nation " ; and he adds, that " a claim to seize them in the streets of London would have been as well founded as that to apprehend them where they were taken," which shows that he has no very correct notions upon the subject. It is readily perceived that no possible question could arise respecting the right to stop the ambassador of your enemy, as you may stop any other enemy, when you find him in the enemy's territory; or if he attempt to pass through your own, on his way to his destination. There is as little doubt that you may not interfere with him while in neutral territory, without just cause of offence to the neutral power whose territory protects him ; and no question whatever that a neutral vessel on the high seas is, as respects belligerent rights, in no just sense neutral territory. The right in time of war to search a neutral vessel which may reasonably be supposed to have contraband goods on board, and to capture and confiscate the vessel, as well as the goods, shows conclusively a marked distinction between the vessel and the territory of the neutral, the latter not being the subject of search, and of course not of seizure and of confiscation, on the ground that munitions of war are found there, — even with evidence that they were intended to be conveyed to the enemy. The question of contraband, or not, does not arise until the goods are on their transit, and out of the local neutral jurisdiction. If then, as a matter of international law, you may stop the ambassador of the enemy, you may stop him on his outward passage while on board a neutral vessel.

But the further question immediately presents itself, May you stop him in all cases where you find him thus in the neutral vessel, and if not, upon what voyage must he be found in order to the exercise of this right? Vattel and the text-writers, in laying down the proposition, could not have contemplated merely the case of a stoppage on a voyage from one port of the enemy to another port belonging to him, because the passage of an ambassador is not ordinarily of that character. Sir William Scott evidently did not so apply it, because he was not speaking with even the most remote reference to any such case. He added, as we have seen, " But when he has arrived, and has taken upon himself the functions of his office " ; showing that the " passage " he had in contemplation was a passage to the place where he was to exercise those functions. This shows also that the principle is not applicable merely to an ambassador returning in a neutral vessel to his own country after his functions have ceased ; nor to the case of an ambassador who, after his reception at the neutral court, is proceeding to another neutral port, for a temporary purpose, on private business, — for that is the very case of all others, if there be one, in which you cannot stop him, because his character of ambassador may be held to continue, and protect him, as if he were still in the neutral country to which he is accredited.

The conclusion would seem to be, that he may be stopped in a neutral vessel, on the high seas, on his way to the country to which he is sent, before his arrival and reception, and before, therefore, he is entitled to the protection of the neutral nation to which he is accredited. And if he may be stopped when proceeding directly from his own port in a neutral vessel, it is not material, so far as the right to stop is concerned, that he has touched at an intermediate port, for the purpose of greater supposed security, and for transshipment. His character of hostility exists as much in the one case as in the other, and it is only when he has arrived in the country in which he is to exercise his office, that this character of hostility ceases, and that of a "*middle*-man," entitled to peculiar privileges, attaches to him, and the neutral territory protects him. But if he is received on board at a neutral port, with no circumstances to excite suspicion that any character of hostility attaches to him, that may well affect the question whether the vessel is liable to confiscation.

It is true that the case of the Caroline was one in which the question related to the carriage of despatches from the Minister and Consul of France in the United States to the government of France ; and it has been objected that the remarks of Sir William Scott on this subject were therefore mere *obiter dicta*, that is, the expression of his opinion. But he was led by the case to consider this very subject, and it is evident from the context and the citation from Vattel, that it was a well-considered opinion. So the text-writers, so far as they speak of the principle, have received it ; for they have promulgated the rule, as thus stated, without doubt or question. At least, we have not seen or heard of anything to the contrary.

We are aware that in the same case Sir William Scott, speaking of despatches, says : —

"The neutral country has a right to preserve its relations with the enemy, and you are not at liberty to conclude that any communication between them can partake in any degree of the nature of hostility against you. The enemy may have his hostile projects to be attempted with the neutral state ; but your reliance is on the integrity of that neutral state, that it will not favor nor participate in such designs, but, as far as its own councils and actions are concerned, will oppose them. And if there should be private reason to suppose that this confidence in the good faith of the neutral state has a doubtful foundation, that is matter for the caution of the government, to be counteracted by just measures of preventive policy, but it is no ground on which this court can pronounce that the neutral carrier has violated his duty by bearing despatches, which, as far as he can know, may be presumed to be of an innocent nature, and in the maintenance of a pacific connection."

But these remarks will not apply to an ambassador for the first time on his passage. If he is proceeding, in time of war, upon an embassy to another nation, even a neutral nation, he goes as a high official, to support the interest of his country there in relation to the war, as well as other matters, and his character is necessarily that of hostility. When he arrives, the neutral territory will protect him; and then perhaps it is not to be presumed that his communications *to the neutral government* are those of hostility, and that you are to place reliance upon the integrity of that government.

We have stated this matter thus at large to show that, on the express statement of the official organ of the Confederate government, these persons were not mere peaceful passengers on their private business, as they seem inclined to represent themselves in their " protest "; and that, if they had possessed the official character which their commissions assumed to confer upon them, they would have been liable to capture.

But these persons were not ambassadors; — no question respecting the rights of an ambassador, or the protection of an ambassador, is brought directly in question by the seizure; — and the case of the United States is all the stronger because they were not entitled to that character.

The right to send an ambassador, and of course to confer the privileges of an ambassador so far as the party sending has the power so to do, is a national right, and not a belligerent right. And as neither the British government, nor any other government, had acknowledged the nationality of the Confederate States, the latter were not authorized to commission an ambassador.

Messrs. Mason and Slidell were public agents of the Confed-

erate States of high official standing, — commissioners, bearers
of despatches to other agents of those States already abroad,
and charged with other errands of hostility to the United
States, — designated as ambassadors, but possessing neither
the character nor the privileges of that office. The general
question then comes, May such hostile agents of the enemy —
proceeding from the enemy's country in an enemy's vessel,
but, for the purpose of avoiding capture, stopping in the territory of one neutral, and there transferring themselves to the
vessel of another neutral — be stopped and captured while
they, with their despatches, are on board the latter vessel,
not having arrived at any territory occupied by that neutral ?
This is the first general question.

It may be admitted that there is no precedent which precisely covers all the facts of this case ; and we are therefore
put upon the inquiry, What is the true principle applicable
to this new state of facts, and by which the question is to
be solved ?

Asking our readers to bear in mind what we have already
stated in regard to the rights, duties, and obligations of neutrals, we proceed to further citations from the opinions and
judgments of Sir William Scott, expressed and rendered in
1807, which were not only binding decisions at the time, deter-
mining the disposition of very large amounts of property, and
then received as sound expositions of law by the British crown
and people, but which have since been generally regarded as
authority by the best elementary writers in England and in this
country.* So far as we are aware, they commanded the entire
confidence of British statesmen and lawyers, until within perhaps the last thirty days. The estimation in which Sir William
Scott was held by the British government appears from the
fact, that he was afterward raised to the peerage, with the title
of Lord Stowell. Our apology for occupying so much of our

---

* See 3 Phill. Int. Law, 368 - 373 ; 1 Kent, 152, 153 ; Wheaton's Int. Law, Part
IV. Chap. 3, Sect. 25.

space with these extracts is, that the volume in which the judgments are published is not of ready access to general readers.

Case of the Orozembo, 6 Robinson's Adm. Rep. 430–439. This was a case of an American vessel,

"that had been ostensibly chartered by a merchant at Lisbon, 'to proceed in ballast to Macao, and there to take a cargo to America,' but which had been afterwards, by his directions, fitted up for the reception of three military officers of distinction, and two persons in civil departments in the government of Batavia, who had come from Holland to take their passage to Batavia, under the appointment of the government of Holland. There were also on board a lady and some persons in the capacity of servants, making in the whole seventeen passengers."

"*Sir William Scott.* . . . . . That a vessel hired by the enemy for the conveyance of military persons is to be considered as a transport subject to condemnation has been in a recent case held by this court, and on other occasions. What is the number of military persons that shall constitute such a case, it may be difficult to define. In the former case there were many, in the present there are much fewer in number; but I accede to what has been observed in argument, that number alone is an insignificant circumstance in the considerations on which the principle of law on this subject is built; since fewer persons of high quality and character may be of more importance than a much greater number of persons of lower condition. To send out one veteran general of France to take the command of the forces at Batavia, might be a much more noxious act than the conveyance of a whole regiment. The consequences of such assistance are greater, and, therefore, it is what the belligerent has a stronger right to prevent and punish. *In this instance the military persons are three; and there are, besides, two other persons, who were going to be employed in civil capacities in the government of Batavia. Whether the principle would apply to them alone, I do not feel it necessary to determine. I am not aware of any case in which the question has been agitated; but it appears to me,* ON PRINCIPLE, *to be but reasonable that, whenever it is of sufficient importance to the enemy that such persons should be sent out on the public service, at the public expense, it should afford equal ground of forfeiture against the vessel that may be let out for a purpose so intimately connected with the hostile operations.*

"It has been argued, that the master was ignorant of the character of the service on which he was engaged, and that, in order to support the penalty, it would be necessary that there should be some proof of delinquency in him, or his owner. But I conceive that is *not* necessary. It will be sufficient if there is an injury arising to the belligerent from the employment in which the vessel is found. In the case of the Swedish vessel there was no *mens rea* in the owner, or in any other person acting under his authority. The master was an involuntary agent, acting under compulsion, put upon him by the officers of the French government, and, so far as intention alone is considered, *perfectly innocent*. In the same manner, in cases of *bona fide* ignorance, there may be no actual delinquency.; but if the service is injurious, that will be sufficient to give the belligerent a right to prevent the thing from being done, or at least repeated, by enforcing the penalty of confiscation. . . . . .

" *If it has appeared to be of sufficient importance to the government of the enemy to send them, it must be enough to put the adverse government on the exercise of their right of prevention.*"

Case of the Atalanta, 6 Rob. Adm. Rep. 440 – 460.

" *Sir William Scott*. . . . . : This being the fact then, that there were on board public despatches of the enemy, not delivered up with the ship's papers, but found concealed, it is incumbent on the persons intrusted with the care of the ship and her cargo to discharge themselves from the imputation of being concerned in the knowledge and management of this transaction. . . . . .

" Not to have pointed them out to the attention of the captors amounts to a fraudulent dissimulation of a fact, which, by the law of nations, he was bound to disclose to those *who had a right to examine, and possess themselves of all papers on board*. . . . . .

" That the simple carrying of despatches between the colonies and the mother country of the enemy is a service highly injurious to the other belligerent, is most obvious. . . . . . It is not to be argued, therefore, that the importance of these despatches might relate only to the civil wants of the colony, and that it is necessary to show a military tendency ; because the object of compelling a surrender being a measure of war, whatever is conducive to that event must also be considered, in the contemplation of law, as an object of hostility, although not produced by operations strictly military. How is this intercourse with the mother country kept up in time of peace? By ships of war, or by packets in the service of the state. If a war intervenes, and the other belligerent prevails to interrupt that communication, any person stepping in to lend himself to effect the same purpose, under the privilege of an ostensible neutral character, does in fact place himself in the service of the enemy state, and is justly to be considered in that character. Nor let it be supposed that it is an act of light and casual importance. The consequence of such a service is indefinite, infinitely beyond the effect of any contraband that can be conveyed. . . . . .

"Unless, therefore, it can be said that there must be a plurality of offences to constitute the delinquency, it has already been laid down by the Superior Court, in the *Constitution*, that fraudulent carrying the despatches of the enemy is a criminal act, which will lead to condemnation. Under the authority of that decision, then, I am warranted to hold, that it is an act which will affect the vehicle, without any fear of incurring the imputation, which is sometimes strangely cast upon this court, that it is guilty of *interpolations* in the laws of nations. If the court took upon itself to assume *principles* in themselves novel, it might justly incur such an imputation ; but to apply established principles to new cases cannot surely be so considered. All law is resolvable into general principles. The cases which may arise under new combinations of circumstances, leading to an extended application of principles, ancient and recognized by just corollaries, may be infinite ; but so long as the continuity of the original and established principles is preserved pure and unbroken, the practice is not *new*, nor is it justly chargeable with being *an innovation* on the ancient law; when, in fact, the court does nothing more than apply old principles to new circumstances. . . . . .

"To talk of the confiscation of the noxious article, *the despatches*, which constitutes the penalty in contraband, would be ridiculous. There would be *no* freight dependent on it, and therefore the same precise penalty cannot, in the nature of things, be applied. It becomes absolutely necessary, as well as just, to resort to some other measure of confiscation, which can be no other than that of the vehicle. . . . . .

"The general rule of law is, that where a party has been *guilty of an interposition in the war*, and is taken *in delicto*, he is not entitled to the aid of the court to obtain the restitution of any part of his property involved in the same transaction. It is said that the term

' interposition in the war ' is a very general term, and not to be loosely applied."

Case of the Susan, 6 Rob. Adm. Rep. 461, note.

" The Susan, an American vessel, captured on a voyage from Bordeaux to New York, having on board a packet addressed to the Prefect of the Isle of France (of which it did not appear that it contained more than a letter, providing for the payment of that officer's salary). The master had made an affidavit, averring his ignorance of the contents, and stating that the packet was delivered to him by a private merchant, as containing old newspapers and some shawls, to be delivered to a merchant at New York. The insignificance of such a communication, and its want of connection with the political objects of the war, were insisted upon. But the court overruled that distinction, under observations similar to those above stated; and on the plea of ignorance observed, that, without saying what might be the effect of a case of extreme imposition practised on a neutral master, notwithstanding the utmost exertions of caution and good faith on his part, it must be taken to be the *general rule*, that a master is not at liberty to aver his ignorance, but that, if he is made the victim of imposition, practised on him by his private agent, or by the government of the enemy, he must seek for his redress against them."

Case of the Caroline, (from which citations have already been made,) 6 Rob. Adm. Rep. 461 – 470.

" This was a case of the same general class as the preceding, on the question of *despatches*, found on board of an American ship, which had been captured with a cargo of cotton and other articles, on freight on a voyage from New York to Bordeaux. In this case the despatches were those of the French Minister and the French Consul in America, going to the departments of government in France."

" *Sir W. Scott.* . . . . . In this case a distinction was taken, very briefly, in the original argument, which I confess struck me very forcibly at the moment, that carrying the despatches of an ambassador, situated in a neutral country, did not fall within the reasoning on which the general principle is founded; and I cannot but say, that the further argument which I have heard on that point, and my own consideration of the subject, have but confirmed the impression which I then received of the solidity of this distinction. . . . . .

"It has been asked, What are despatches? To which, I think, this answer may safely be returned: that they are all official communications of official persons on the public affairs of the government. The comparative importance of the particular papers is immaterial, since the court will not construct a scale of relative importance, which in fact it has not the means of doing, with any degree of accuracy, or with satisfaction to itself. It is sufficient, that they relate to the public business of the enemy, be it great or small. . . . . . It is not to be said, therefore, that this or that letter is of small moment; the true criterion will be, Is it on the public business of the state, and passing between public persons for the public service? *That* is the question. . . . . . But if the papers so taken relate to public concerns, be they great or small, civil or military, the court will not split hairs, and consider their relative importance. . . . . .

"The circumstances of the present case, however, do not bring it within the range of these considerations, because it is not the case of despatches coming from any port of the enemy's territory, whose *commerce* and communications of every kind the other belligerent has a right to interrupt. They are despatches from persons who are in a peculiar manner the favorite objects of the protection of the law of nations, *ambassadors*, resident in a neutral country, for the purpose of preserving the relations of amity between that state and his own government. . . . . .

"It has been argued truly, that, whatever the necessities of the negotiation may be, a private merchant is under no obligation to be the carrier of the enemy's despatches to his own country. Certainly he is not: and one inconvenience, to which he may be held fairly subject, is that of having his vessel brought in for examination, and of the necessary detention and expense. He gives the captors an undeniable right to intercept and examine the nature and contents of the papers which he is carrying; for they *may* be papers of an injurious tendency, although not such, on any *a priori* presumption, as to subject the party who carries them to the penalty of confiscation, and by giving the captors the right of that inquiry, he must submit to all the inconvenience that may attend it. Ship and cargo restored *on payment of captors' expense.*"

It will be found, we think, from a careful examination of these opinions, that the general principle applicable to the case is, that the subject or citizen of the neutral nation may not do anything directly auxiliary to the warlike purposes of a belligerent, or, as it is expressed in other words, anything which has a direct tendency to promote his warlike operations ; and that the transportation of agents whose business is to promote or facilitate any hostile operations, or of despatches which have, or may be presumed to have, a hostile character, is a rendition of aid to the belligerent which justifies the capture of the persons and despatches, and if done with knowledge, actual or constructive, is such a violation of neutrality as authorizes the capture and confiscation of the neutral vessel.

Speaking of the right of search, it has been said : " The only security that nothing is to be found inconsistent with amity and the law of nations is the right of personal visitation and search, to be exercised by those who have an interest in making it." We have here another expression of the general principle which regulates neutral rights and duties. It is not merely that the neutral is not warranted in carrying this or that article, or this or that person. He is not to carry anything which is inconsistent with the amity which subsists between his nation and the belligerent, and which he should maintain toward the belligerent.

Having ascertained the principles which are applicable, we turn again to the facts of this case. Probably no one doubts that Messrs. Mason and Slidell were the public agents of the Confederate States, charged with all manner of duties of a belligerent character. But Great Britain may reasonably ask for some evidence of the fact, as a justification for their removal from the Trent. The proof will doubtless be found to be abundant, but our space permits only two or three suggestions. In the first place, there is the message of Mr. Davis, in which he states that they are commissioned, and speaks of them as " Ministers," showing them to be public agents for the promotion of the interests of the revolutionary government.

In the next place, there is a conclusive presumption that their agency was of a belligerent character, because the people of the Confederate States, being in rebellion, waging a civil war, and acknowledged only as a belligerent power, whatever is to be done for their success is necessarily of a belligerent character. The voyage of their agents to Europe was " directly auxiliary to the warlike purposes " of the Confederacy, and as hostile as if they had been officers or soldiers on their way to aid the enemy. An attempt merely to procure an acknowledgment of the independence of the Confederate States, while the United States are surrounding them with forces by land and sea, is of itself an act of hostility to the United States. The object could only be encouragement and aid in the prosecution of the war, as there is no practical independence.

Similar remarks apply to the despatches. That such documents were on board is not now concealed. The failure of Captain Wilkes to find them has been a matter of exultation. Lieutenant Fairfax was not bound to search for them after the captain of the Trent refused to show his passenger list or to give any information. He might well suppose that they were then beyond reasonable search, perhaps concealed by some of the ladies connected with the agency, in what the Boston Post, speaking of the secret transmission of traitorous correspondence by Secession ladies in the vicinity of Washington, termed "the holy precincts of their nether garments." The Confederate States had no minister, nor any consul, in Europe ; but they had agents there actively attempting to procure an acknowledgment of their independence, and engaged in purchasing and transmitting munitions of war to the Southern ports. The despatches, then, must be presumed to relate to these subjects.

The fact that the voyage of the neutral vessel was from one

9

neutral port to another would not have exempted these persons from capture, even if they had been ambassadors from a recognized nation, their mission being of a hostile character. *A fortiori*, it cannot exempt them when they are mere agents. The character of hostility which necessarily attaches to them as the public agents of a mere belligerent power, proceeding with despatches which from the nature of the case must be presumed to be to hostile agents and for hostile purposes, shows a right to capture them, even if an ambassador might be exempted on such a voyage because he was a "*middle-man*." We have the distinct opinion of Sir William Scott that the transportation of civilians may be ground of forfeiture.

The neutral vessel was rendering aid in the accomplishment of these hostile purposes, just as much as she would have been if her voyage had been direct from the belligerent port. The neutral right, therefore, cannot protect the hostile agent, whether there was or was not knowledge. The want of knowledge might protect the vessel. But here was ample evidence to charge the captain of the Trent with full knowledge of the character of hostility; and it may probably be shown that the embarkation at Havana was with sufficient pomp and circumstance to constitute plenary evidence, if there were no other.*

The Trent was a private passenger packet, with the advantage of a contract to carry the mails. She was a common carrier of passengers, and perhaps of goods also, but had no more of the character of a government vessel than the railroad car which carries the mail and the mail-agent, under a contract with the postmaster-general, has the character of a government vehicle. She was therefore liable, under the circumstances, to capture, and to confiscation also.

But here comes another, and it would seem, from recent suggestions, the main point to be considered. The Trent was

---

* See Appendix, Note B.

not captured. It is said that for this reason the proceedings are all irregular, and that a demand for a delivery of the prisoners is to be made by the British government, founded upon the neglect to make the capture, and the consequent lack of any proof of a right to take the persons. This is quite too narrow a view of the matter, and we shall not believe, until we have demonstrative assurance, that the law officers of the Crown will place themselves upon such a small and slippery foundation. We shall not enlarge upon the ill grace with which Great Britain would urge the objection, not that Mason and Slidell could not be taken, but that Captain Wilkes did not capture the steamer, send her in for trial and confiscation, and in so doing delay her Majesty's mails, and derange the business of all the passengers and others concerned in the regular trip of the vessel, — that there was therefore no adjudication of a prize court to show that the persons could be captured, and no other evidence would be received. Nor need we show what a gross outrage it would be to fasten a quarrel upon the nation whose officer had been guilty of such an act of comity and favor. If blood ever cries to Heaven for vengeance, it would be the blood shed in a war having such a foundation. And if all Christendom did not cry, Shame! it would show that the part of it which failed in the performance of that duty to humanity had lost all consciousness of the difference between right and wrong. Such a failure to do Great Britain an injury may possibly be made a *pretext* for war. It can never be the foundation of a *point of honor*, requiring an apology.

But it is argued, that in no other way than by sending in the vessel can it be shown by regular proof that the right to seize these persons existed; and therefore, that, by reason of the failure to send in the vessel, we cannot establish the right of seizure. It is alleged that it has always been the law of the world, that every cruiser making a seizure on board of a vessel shall bring the vessel in, and subject the lawfulness of the seizure to adjudication in a prize court; and that there is one excuse only, and that is a want of force on the part of the captors to man the prize. Very well, we have one case, then, in which it is not necessary to establish the right to seize, by the decision of a prize court. Now suppose that Captain Wilkes had seized the despatches, and, taking them and Messrs. Mason and Slidell on board of the San Jacinto, (as we suppose he had a right to do, for safety, if he had a right to seize the Trent,) had then put a prize crew on board of her, and that she had afterward foundered at sea, or been captured by a Confederate privateer. The proceedings in admiralty for confiscation are *in rem;* and the *thing* being gone, no evidence of the right to seize could be had through the adjudication of a prize court. This would not have discharged the persons, nor forfeited the right to withhold the despatches. Here, then, seems to be another case.

We readily admit that the officer making a seizure cannot confiscate the property. If a judgment of confiscation is sought, the property must be libelled. The vessel is sent in as prize, and because she is prize, and is to be disposed of as prize; and not because she is necessary as evidence. Evidence other than that found on board the vessel may be received. (6 Robinson, 351, Case of the Romeo.)

But we have seen by the opinion of Sir William Scott, that *despatches are not the subject of confiscation; and it is at least equally clear that Messrs. Mason and Slidell are not so. If the vessel had been sent in, there could not have been any proceeding in the prize court against them or the despatches, and of course no judgment against either.* It is true that, the violation of neutrality by the transportation of the persons and of the despatches being the alleged ground of the seizure and of the claim of forfeiture, the question whether the persons were to be regarded as hostile agents, whether the despatches were of a hostile character, and all other questions affecting the right to seize, would be directly before the court, and would be determined there, *for the purposes of that case; that is, for the purpose of deciding whether the vessel was liable to confiscation or seizure, but no further. The judgment of the prize court would not operate upon the persons or papers.* While, upon the ordinary principles of law, in the absence of fraud or gross mistake, Great Britain would be bound to respect and abide by the decree of the court, so far as regarded the vessel, as the United States have done in relation to the decisions of Sir William Scott, there would be nothing in the judgment of the court to prevent that government from claiming of the United States the persons and papers, on evidence to be adduced in support of the claim, if it was believed that the opinion of the prize court was erroneous.

The distinction between evidence necessary to prove an issue, and the matter in issue, is familiar to every sound lawyer. A man is indicted for stealing the property of A. B., and in order to procure a conviction it must be proved, to the satisfaction of the jury, that the property alleged to have been stolen was the property of A. B., and this being done, the defendant is convicted. But this will not prevent C. D. from afterward sustaining a suit, to recover the property or its value, on evidence that it in fact belonged to him. It may be said that the reason is, that C. D. was not a party to the proceedings under the indictment, and so not bound by the proceeding there; but that in the prize court, where the proceedings are *in rem*, all persons interested in the property are regarded as parties, and bound by the decree. Admit it. But they are parties only as to the matter in issue, and not as to the evidence; and they are bound therefore only so far as the judgment goes, that is, by the confiscation of the vessel.

We claim, then, to have shown that the seizure, and even the confiscation, of the vessel would have determined nothing in relation to Messrs. Mason and Slidell, except for the purpose of the inquiry, Prize or not prize? that the judgment in the prize court would in no wise have operated upon them; and that the opinion which that court entertained, so far from being conclusive on the British government in relation to their capture, would not, in a legal point of view, be even *prima facie* evidence. In a diplomatic correspondence between that government and the United States, it might, if it existed, be used as evidence; but other evidence would be equally admissible on either side. · On the other hand, the judgment of the prize court releasing the vessel, based upon the expressed opinion of the judge that the persons were not liable to capture, and that the neutral vessel was in the regular exercise of her rights, while it may have furnished ground for an application to the government for their discharge, would not have been legal evidence of a right to their liberty.

We maintain, therefore, that all questions respecting the legality of the seizure of persons on board of neutral vessels, so far as they affect the persons themselves, or the relations of the government to which they belong and that making the seizure, are either legal questions for courts of common-law jurisdiction, or political questions to be settled by negotiation, if they can be settled in that mode.

If these positions are correct, the conclusion cannot be escaped that the capture of the vessel was not necessary, either as matter of substance or of form, in order to justify the capture of the persons. "*Lex neminem cogit ad vana seu inutilia.*" "*Utile per inutile non vitiatur.*"

But it may be asked, Has the captain of a belligerent cruiser a right to overhaul the merchant-vessel of a neutral nation, and take men out of her, on the plea that they are enemies, without any adjudication as to the right to make the capture? We answer, Certainly, if he can make proof of the right afterward. There can be no adjudication at the time. He does it on his responsibility and the responsibility of his government, if the right cannot be established. If he may seize vessel, crew, cargo, and passengers on this responsibility, and send them all into port, surely he may seize the hostile passengers who give occasion for the capture. In fact, if Captain Wilkes had seized the vessel, it would have been his duty to take Messrs. Mason and Slidell on board his own vessel for security, and on his arrival to report, and deliver them into the custody of the government, which might at once have released them, and this without affecting the proceedings against the vessel.

Further, a party who has a right may waive that right; certainly, if others are not thereby prejudiced. The only parties interested in favor of the capture of the Trent were the United States and the officers and crew of the San Jacinto. Captain Wilkes, in behalf of the United States, and for himself, his officers, and crew, waived the right to make the capture; and the government has sanctioned that proceeding. Is Great Britain prejudiced?

The speeches at the banquet of the Lord Mayor of London certainly did not indicate a rupture of the friendly relations between the United States and Great Britain within a very short period; but it must be admitted that this furnishes no absolute assurance.

If Great Britain insists upon the delivery up of the prisoners, and the Cabinet at Washington surrender them *upon the ground that the demand is a distinct abandonment of the doctrines which she and her prize courts have heretofore so persistently maintained*, the people will acquiesce, and she may yet believe that she has gained nothing by the course thus pursued. If she demand an apology because *the United States have merely followed out those doctrines*, we venture the opinion that she will not get it.

APPENDIX.

Note A. Page 32.

The United States have for a long period, in treaties and otherwise, endeavored to procure the introduction of certain principles into the law of nations, different from those heretofore held by Great Britain, respecting the rights of neutrals, — among them, the principle that the neutral flag should cover the property of an enemy not contraband of war. The Congress at Paris in 1856 adopted this with other principles; and the United States having offered to become a party to that adoption, the principle may perhaps be recognized hereafter, although the accession of the United States to the declaration of the Congress at Paris has not been received.

Note B. Page 66.

The following extracts show that Dr. Phillimore recognizes the right of the belligerent to search and seize where the voyage is from one neutral port to another neutral port. He puts that as a case where there is less to excite the vigilance of the master of the neutral vessel, and one where some allowance should be made for any imposition practised on him.

"It is indeed competent to those intrusted with the care of the ship on board of which such despatches are found, to discharge themselves from the imputation of being concerned in the knowledge or management of the transaction. But the presumption is strong against the ignorance of the master of the ship; and when he has knowingly taken on board a packet or letter addressed to a public officer of a belligerent government, the plea of the insig-

10

nificance of the communication, and its want of connection with the political objects of the war, will not avail him; nor, except perhaps in an extreme case of imposition practised upon him, will the plea of ignorance of the *contents* of the despatches avail him : his redress must be sought against the person whose agent or carrier he was.

"With respect to such a case as might exempt the carrier of despatches from the usual penalty, it is to be observed that *where the commencement of the voyage is in a neutral country, and to terminate at a neutral port,* or at a port to which, though not neutral, an open trade is allowed, in such case there is less to excite the vigilance of the master; and therefore it may be proper to make some allowance for any imposition which may be practised on him. But where the neutral master receives papers on board in a hostile port, he receives them at his own hazard, and cannot be heard to avow his ignorance of a fact with which, by due inquiry, he might have made himself acquainted." — 3 *Phill. Int. Law,* 374 (published in 1857).

It may be admitted that in such case, if, without knowledge on the part of the master, and with nothing to excite suspicion, he, in the ordinary course of his business, carries contraband goods intended for a belligerent, or the officers, soldiers, agents, or despatches of a belligerent, this should not furnish cause for the confiscation of the vessel. But neither the fact that the immediate transit was from one neutral port to another, nor the want of knowledge of the master, furnishes a reason why the contraband goods intended for the belligerent, or the persons in his service, or his despatches, should have active transportation, for the purposes of the war, by the neutral vessel, and at the same time immunity from capture because of her neutrality. The vessel cannot be regarded as the *territory* of the neutral under such circumstances, for territory is not a vehicle of transportation.

www.ingramcontent.com/pod-product-compliance
Lightning Source LLC
Chambersburg PA
CBHW030020030726
47499CB00008B/3059